From the Chronicles of Cosmic History

T5-BQB-073

To Mars To Stay

To Mars To Die

Plus Bonus Short Story

"Hello I, This is H."

By Bill M. Tracer

First Edition

Cosmographic Publishing
Knoxville, TN 37922

Cosmographic Publishing
info@cosmographic.com
Knoxville, TN 37922

Printed in the United States of America

ISBN-13: 978-1500281823

First Edition

Dedication

To David Edward Jones, without your contribution to my consciousness, my work would be all the poorer. To say your ceaseless imagination has enhanced boundlessly my own, would be little short of an utter understatement.

Disclaimer

The Cover art is an original creation by the author, using a combination of NASA's public domain image of Mars, (also used on the cover page), layer blended, and photo color enhanced, then utilized as a material application to a virtual 3D object and rendered into the outer space scene using the 3D program, Bryce 7.1.

All characters and beings in this book are fictional. Similarities to anyone or any entities in actual reality are coincidental, and not intended to offend. Perceived slights or snubs toward any individuals or organizations are completely unintentional. The information provided in this book is set forth with the express understanding that it is a work of science fiction, and makes no extraordinary claims to contain any business, financial, legal, or other type of professional advice. If you're seeking such services, you should consult the appropriate professionals.

Regarding any external hyperlinks sited in this work: These links are provided as a convenience and for informational purposes only; they do not constitute an endorsement or approval by the publisher or writer of this work, of any of the products, services or opinions of the corporations or organizations or individuals. The publisher bears no responsibility for the long term accuracy, efficacy, legality or content of the external sites or for that of subsequent links, or for any problems arising from their use. Please contact the external sites for answers to any questions regarding their content.

Table of Contents

Acknowledgments

First of all, I want to thank those whose contributions to the effort of this novella and bonus short story were both invaluable and essential. To all of you I give a hearty nod and thanks.

A special acknowledgement goes to David Edward Jones, and David Bryan Nichols, my co-creators of the shared Cosmographic Universe in which both this novella and the bonus short story take place.

A special thanks to NASA for providing so many of their beautiful images for public domain free usage, such as the image of Mars, (known as "Mars planet of the solar system"), used to adorn this work of science fiction. For more information about this and other public domain images see: http://www.public-domain-image.com/space-public-domain-images-pictures/mars-planet-of-the-solar-system.jpg.html

To my beta readers, your part in the creation of this work goes beyond indispensable. Without your input, this would be a far less rich work.

Prologue:
They Will Return To Stay

Deep Subsurface of Mars: AD 2043

Deep in submarinean chambers Martian Myripods communed telepathically with one another, as they had for many millennia. They established a great communion collectively as if one boundless mind. Together, they watched events unfolding far above them, on the long uninhabitable surface, as the last of the human invaders lifted off from their Valles Marineris Base. They left in place several structures, and robots busily extracting oxygen from Mars' rusty sands.

'They leave. Yes, to their Earth they return home. But their intensions remain clear. They will come back, and if their trends continue, they will eventually return to stay.'

In the cavernous halls of the Martian collective, a shutter cascaded throughout the Myripod Overmind.

'They will return to stay.'

The Overmind divided into questions, and recombined to seek answers.

Division one asked, 'What will be our response?'

Division two added, 'Should not our response be swift?'

Division three interjected, 'But would it not be prudent for us to measure every action for appropriateness? Are not the ancient treaties still in place?'

Division four exploded, 'Even if so, is not their invasion of our surface enough violation to render the ancient treaties void?

Recombined, 'These we must contemplate.'

Chapter 1:
The Breathtaking View

Valles Marineris, Mars: AD 2047

Eric Sheffield stood at a rocky outcropping overlooking Eos Chasma. The huge gorge, near the eastern end of Valles Marineris, stretched before him imposingly. By comparison, this enormous valley made the Grand Canyon of Earth look like a small riverbed. The weather lingered calm that day. Eric noticed a diminutive dust cloud momentarily lift, and then drift far off within the deep ravine. Like those shifting Martian sands, his mind wandered in placid reverie, soaking up the breathtaking view.

Absentmindedly he modified his helmet visor magnification, zooming in on the Eos bottoms. His grey eyes adjusted. There it came again; that all too familiar apprehension. It felt as though someone watched him. For nearly two years, this foreboding had plagued Eric, ever since their mission arrived in Martian orbit in AD 2045. He couldn't discern who or what it might be, but the feeling remained relentless.

Eric's mind momentarily returned to the first time this wary feeling of being watched had seized him. He then stood looking out his favorite view port on the VM crew module. This crew module was one of three attached to the expedition vessel, "Marco Polo". Their trinary craft arrived much later than her sister vessels, on this Mars mission. Five months earlier, meteor fragments damaged Marco Polo's solar wind sails, and slowed their journey. When they finally entered Martian orbit, Eric remembered being quite anxious to see Mars from above. He watched intently as their spinning craft passed over the fourth planet's rusty sands. He wondered if the popular theory might be true. Had life once resided there? As if in reply, he heard a soft whisper in the back of his mind, 'More have arrived.'

Startled, Eric looked over his shoulder. Hilda approached, gazing fondly at him, her round face filled with a smile.

He asking, "What did you say?"

Hilda replied, "Nothing, I didn't say anything."

Eric laughed nervously, and ran bony fingers through thin brown hair, "I could have sworn I heard a whisper, 'More have arrived.' Did you hear it?"

At the portal, Hilda bumped Eric's hip with her own to move him over, affording herself a view. Small of frame, Eric easily moved. Hilda replied with a shrug, "Well, it wasn't me. What a view?"

Eric turned back from Hilda to the portal, "It is beautiful, but the Marco Polo's revolutions keep it spinning. I guess it made me dizzy."

Hilda returned lighthearted, "Don't worry about it, Eric. It's been a long trip for all of us. I'm just glad we're here. If it had gone on much longer, we'd all be hearing things; maybe even seeing things too. Who knows, we could've all thought imaginary Martians were out to get us."

He tried to shrug it off, but it nagged at him. It floated near the edge of his awareness, and refused capture by full perception, while Hilda's dismissive laughter threatened to distract his attention from this covert surveillance. Someone or something watched them. It worried Eric. It kept returning, like that day, as Eric looked deep into Eos Chasma.

Eric glanced behind his shoulder, but saw nothing to explain his anxiety. He swiveled his entire suited body away from the valley but still nothing, only the rover a few meters away.

Chapter 2:
Thank you, Galadriel

Entrenched far below Eric's feet in subsurface caverns Myripod Martians studied the Earth human invaders, who then desecrated the uninhabitable surface of their world. Slowly, they contemplated their appropriate response.

They knew Eric sensed their extrasensory scrutiny. They marveled that he seemed mostly unconscious of his own psychic potential. Without trying, he could discern their far sighted examinations of him, and his fellow invaders. The need for another distraction had once again arisen.

Humans must not discover their secret presence; not yet. Perhaps in time, depending on the results of their current analysis. The appropriate response seemed so elusive, for though they shared in the fullness of mental collectivity, they were diverse of mind, constantly debating, rarely finding consensus, of late. However, on the issue of distracting the human sensitive, Eric, they remained resolute and uncharacteristically of one mind.

Eric's helmet radio headgear filled with a loud static pop.

He clinched his fist, and grit his teeth. Anger griped him. This old wrath lingered; older than Eric himself understood. It suited the needs of the Myripod Martians, though they couldn't comprehend it's true meaning. They found this anger deep in Eric's mind, not long after the VM crew arrived. For them, it continued to be an easy matter to pull this deep unanswered anger to the surface of Eric's mind. Once there, it blocked his perceptions of their psychic espionage. They neglected to consider any potential side effects this practice might bring on.

His grandfather's words, from long ago, echoed in Eric's mind, "Never trust the top dogs. They'd just as soon lead you astray, as not, if it suits their needs. Always try to find that place where your needs and their needs meet. That's when we all get along."

Eric inherited his grandfather's resentment of authority. Unfortunately, he ranked seventh in the command hierarchy at Valles Marineris Base, with a crew compliment of seven. Eric had only the computers and robots to give orders, and he found small consolation in that. The stress of being on the bottom rung drove Eric from VM Base to solitary explorations of surrounding Martian landscapes. These scouting missions were part of his official role, but he did them more frequently than required, just to get a little peace from incessant orders, and Hilda's unwanted advances.

Eric slowly walked back to VM Mars Rover 01, affectionately dubbed "Galadriel".

Briefly he focused on the persistent quiet hiss of air within his suit's life support system. It yielded the desired calming effect. That shift of mental focus served like an almost walking meditation.

Eric gave an order, "Galadriel, open your pressure hatch." His tone came out sharper than he'd meant. He took another deep breath and entered the rover's hatch. Automatically, he initiated interior pressurization.

Galadriel's artificial feminine computer voice spoke into Eric's ear through helmet COMM link. She said, "Welcome back on board, Eric. Pressurization of VM Mars Rover 01 has begun. Pressurization will be complete in three minutes. Please stand by, Eric."

Eric sat at Galadriel's control panel, and prepared for helmet removal. He casually unscrewed the securing clamps.

"Pressurization of VM Mars Rover 01 is now complete. Your environment suit may be removed," Galadriel informed him.

"Thank you, Galadriel," Eric said plainly.

He pushed down and gave his helmet a twist to the right. This disconnected the helmet from the rest of his suit.

Equipped with a pair of retractable robot arms from directly over Eric's head, Galadriel could carry out the same task, but Eric preferred doing it himself. The robotic method took far too much time. By contrast, he allowed Galadriel to assist with the next step. Swiveling to the right, he inserted his arms into two receptacles right of the control panel and ordered, "Galadriel, detach."

Small clamps locked onto the environment suit sleeves, disengaged them, and gently sucked them from around his arms, into the mechanism. Eric simply removed his arms from the receptacles, then adorned with only the sleeves of the standard light blue jumper, worn under his environment suit.

Eric felt it easier to stop at this point, not removing the entire suit every time, though Galadriel always stood by ready and perfectly capable of robotically assisting him with complete suit removal and reattachment.

"Galadriel, give me a topographic map of the surrounding lands. Detail a thirty kilometer radius around VM Base."

The commanded data appeared on the rover's main view screen. As ordered, the map revealed a circular area of topography, sixty km in diameter. The graphic resolution popped with marvelous detail.

Eric could see Valles Marineris Base marked with a black dot at the circle's center. The initial view came up from overhead by default, but could easily be adjusted to any perspective panorama.

Eric's eyes roamed about the map. He added, "Replace grid 698 over explored areas. Mark current location."

Galadriel complied, "Gladly, Eric."

A white grid superimposed over the topographic map. A tiny flashing green diamond marked the current location of the rover.

"Thank you Galadriel. Now please plot course to the nearest location outside explored grid. Indicate course in flashing yellow," Eric further commanded.

Giving commands felt good. He maintained an acute awareness that Galadriel and the other AIs, were the only entities he could do that with. At least he had them.

Eric stared at a slightly curved flashing yellow line.

"All right Galadriel", Eric instructed, "please extend the course east one more kilometer beyond explored grid, and mark projected destination with red X."

Satisfied with the final results, Eric sat back, strapped in, gave the map one last overall inspection, and finally after a long pause, which would have made any other human in his presence uncomfortable, but had no effect on Galadriel's judgment, he said, "Initiate plotted course."

Chapter 3:
To Mars To Stay

The rover lightly jerked into motion.

"Primary view screen, forward vista mode, please," Eric commanded hastily.

The map disappeared. In its place he saw a wide panoramic perspective view of the Martian landscape, stretching before Rover 01. Though not necessary, Eric preferred to see where the rover traveled. It gave him a feeling of greater control. After pressing a short sequence of touch pads, Eric displayed the map on a smaller screen. The blinking green diamond slowly moved along the flashing yellow line. The line behind the diamond changed from yellow to red, indicating course already traversed.

Under the rover's tread, a large rock gave way. A minor rockslide resulted. The rover lunged uncomfortably to Eric's left. He quickly shifted his attention from map, back to primary view screen. The rover left behind the predominantly sandy environment overlooking Eos, and entered a region littered with increased rocky rubble. Eric heard and felt the vibration of small rocks clinking through the sand filtration system.

"Galadriel, disengage sand sifters, and report!" Eric snapped.

The hollow hissing sound of the sand sifters ceased. The rover slowed to about half its standard speed.

Galadriel stated the obvious. "The rover has entered a zone with a greater than average distribution of rocky debris. Standard procedure is to slow the rover's speed appropriately. This step has been taken."

Eric considered this report inadequate.

"What about the sand sifters? Any filter damage from those rocks?" Eric inquired.

Galadriel said, "Self diagnostics in progress. Please stand by, Eric."

The standing by lasted longer than Eric liked. Finally, Galadriel continued, "Self diagnostics complete. No functional damage detected."

Eric sighed, and whispered, "That's a relief."

He carefully watched the primary view screen. A quick glance at the map showed the green indicator approaching the explored grid's edge. The Martian landscape stretching before him revealed little variance. Eric relaxed. He allowed his mind to drift back in time. He remembered the day, when they left L2 space station. Four transport vessels left that day, all designed with three landing modules. Each transport vessel had a crew of three, with all of their adjoined landing modules containing seven crewmembers, so a total of ninety-six human beings embarked that day bound for Mars. They were not the first to go there. This was in fact the third Earth to Mars mission. But these intrepid explorers had been assigned the honor of first to remain, establishing a permanent human presence on Mars. The catch phrase of their mission, and repeated incessantly by all media the world over rang out, "To Mars to Stay."

Three of the twelve landing sites would retain a crew until four years later a relief crew would replace some of them, and otherwise add to the base populations. Several years earlier, the first mission to Mars established three landing sites, stayed for two years, and returned to Earth, leaving behind equipment and structures. The second mission reinforced the original three sites, and established six new sites. After two and a half years, they too returned to Earth. The current mission returned to the nine existing bases, established three new ones, with the three oldest sites to be made permanent bases. Eric felt privileged, a crewmember bound for the enduring base site at Valles Marineris. He could still see the view through Marco Polo's portal, as the Earth slowly receded into its black backdrop speckled with myriad stars.

The AI computer voice brought back his wondering mind, when Galadriel said, "VM Mars Rover 01 has now passed out of previously explored areas."

"Good," Eric said, scanning the landscape. "Thank you, Galadriel."

Before him, Eric could see more rocks, and sand with a decidedly rusty color. Slowly the rover rumbled over Mars' rocky land. It all looked much the same. Rocks and sand, sand and rocks, little else stretched before him.

Once again the AI computer interrupted his thoughts, "VM Mars Rover 01 is passing into a slowly slopping crater concavity. Upon reaching the designated coordinates the rover will be temporarily out of transmission range to and from VM Base. Communication must not be cut off more than one hour. Automatic alert measures will be implemented at VM Base if transmissions do not resume within the indicated time, Eric."

Eric nodded, "I understand, Galadriel. We won't be here that long."

The rover came to a gradual stop.

Chapter 4:
Extreme Caution Advised, Eric

Eric disconnected his seat strap.

"Okay, Galadriel let's do a standard full panoramic view of our surroundings," Eric ordered.

He leaned in close as he watched the high resolution screen stretch out that panoramic view. This Marscape was not as impressive as the view he enjoyed earlier, overlooking Eos Chasma, but it had its own appeal and one mild curiosity. In the midst of these scattered rocks, stood one lone sand dune. There's nothing unusual about a sand dune on Mars. Eric had viewed plenty, but this one stood out in an otherwise rocky environment. It seemed strangely misplaced and oddly shaped. He found himself hard pressed to put his finger on just what might be amiss, but something appeared out of sorts about this particular dune.

He ordered, "Galadriel, please focus your cameras at uh, where is that, uh 34.8 degrees off panoramic center. Let's get a closer look at that odd shaped sand dune. Zoom in 10 X."

Absent-mindedly, while still gazing intently at the screen, he turned his body to the right and inserted his arms into the sleeve / glove attachment receptacles. He ordered, "Galadriel, please re-engage environment suit sleeves."

Galadriel's robotic mechanisms within went right to work, reattaching the sleeves of his environment suit. But this barely registered in Eric's attention, for he stared at that peculiar mound of sand on Galadriel's view screen

Reflective glare hit his eye. It came from a jagged object emerging from a depression on the right. It looked like burnished metal; some torn piece of a manufactured object.

"Is that metal?" Eric muttered to himself, as he removed his then fully suited arms from the receptacles.

Eric wonder, maybe it's the old Seeker roving robot, from the early 21st Century, Probe? It landed near the later VM Base site. First base crew retrieved the lander, but Seeker itself had yet to be found.

"Scanning, please stand by, Eric," Galadriel responded as if Eric's metal question had been for her.

He considered correcting the misunderstanding, but thought better of it. He hesitated, awaiting data from Galadriel. He didn't have a long wait.

"The dune is composed of 90.258 % metallic alloys. There is a hollow chamber surrounded by a metallic shell, which is in turn covered with a thin coating of fine Martian sand. Traces of organic matter are present within the chamber. Extreme caution advised, Eric, "Galadriel warned with artificial concern. Her worried tone seemed almost real, but Eric knew better.

"Organic matter," He exclaimed! "Is there anything alive in there, now?"

Galadriel replied, "Sensors show organic matter inert, with no indications of current life, Eric. However, if you intend to investigate, I maintain a recommendation for extreme caution."

Excited, Eric returned, "Your warning is noted, but it's not going to stop me."

Eric re-engaged his helmet. He made sure all attachments were secure, and checked the air gages inside the helmet. Everything appeared in order, so Eric commanded, "Galadriel, please de-pressurize the rover."

Galadriel's familiar feminine voice replied, "De-pressurization of VM Mars Rover 01 has begun. De-pressurization will be complete in three minutes. Please be sure your environment suit is functioning properly Eric; then stand by."

The low hiss of air could be both heard and felt. Eric stood by.

"De-pressurization of VM Rover 01 is complete. You may open the hatch, and disembark, Eric," Galadriel said with perfect intonation, but no real emotion.

He tripped the securing latch. Galadriel opened the hatch. Without hesitation, Eric stepped out and surveyed the surrounding rocky sand. He could clearly see the crater's gradual slope. He approached the lone dune, hurriedly at first, slowing to a more cautious pace the closer he got to it.

His thoughts rushed with uncharacteristic exhilaration, 'It must be a crashed space ship. What else could it be?'

He stopped just before the depression. Carefully he brushed aside sand from this depression's jagged lip. The sand yielded, revealing a metallic surface.

Eric backed up a step, when the full realization finally hit deep into his mind that this depression represented a gaping hole leading inside what Galadriel described as a metallic shell. This mound of sand surely covered a crashed spacecraft, and he might be able to enter it through this hole. His heart raced.

He knocked away more sand from around the depression. The sand gave way with ease. Much of it collapsed into the depression itself, revealing a large breech in the ship's hull. Eric could see directly into the alien spacecraft. And yes, it was alien, not the

Seeker rover or anything else human made. The opening sat there before his eyes, big enough for him to get through, provided he stooped.

Recklessly, Eric stepped inside.

Near the breach, he saw a small mummified body. Not human, but Eric knew exactly what kind of body he gazed upon. In 2024 these small grey beings made themselves officially known to the citizens of Earth. Unofficially, they had been around for thousands of years, covertly making subtle genetic alterations to Earth human genome. They're known on Earth as Zeta Reticulans, in keeping with their claim of inhabiting two planets in the binary star system Zeta Reticula A and B, though some assert they've lost at least one of those "home worlds" to an unknown enemy.

Eric looked around the inner chamber. Cramped space forced him to remain stooped.

Three other mummified bodies lay within sight.

A reflective glint caught his eye. Next to the hand of one mummified Zeta Reticulan rested a rod shaped tool. Eric moved closer. It looked like a small wand. Except for being a bit longer, it reminded Eric of a laser pointer used by academy lecturers. He retrieved it, and turned it slowly in his gloved hand. It appeared featureless, with neither buttons nor any visible mechanisms; its surface polished smooth and highly reflective. Two deep black, long mummified eyes stared back at Eric, as his focus shifted from the tool to its surface reflection. A strange urge seized him. He lifted the wand, pointing one end toward his helmet.

Abruptly everything changed, though it seemed perfectly normal, to him. A young boy again, he sat at the edge of a pond, fishing with his grandfather.

"I remember this day." Eric said with youthful enthusiasm.

"Don't believe everything you see. And you can only believe in what can be proven," his grandfather said angrily.

Young Eric stammered, "I... I don't understand, Grandfather."

"Of course you don't! You never will," Came the old man's gruff reply. He leaned close to Eric, their faces almost touching, "You found something, did you?"

"Yes," Eric said happily, lifting his fishing pole transformed into the wand. He continued to hold it as if it were still his fishing pole. "Do you know what it is, Grandfather?"

"It's a Grey tool. You shouldn't play with it. We should never trust the Greys, you know", Eric's grandfather said sternly.

"But, Grandfather, they helped us. They helped us clean up from the calamity. Were it not for them, we would've destroyed ourselves with the almost nuclear war back in 2024."

"Yes, Eric, they helped us. They've got their own reasons. It's not because they're our friends. That's certain. You can count on it. For all we know they could have caused the calamity themselves, to soften us up so they could come along a few months later, and claim to be our friends and help us right into being their pawns."

Eric's grandfather leaned back abruptly, as his fishing pole jerked. With a jolt of the pole, he started reeling in his catch.

Eric remained confused.

"But, Grandfather," he said, "I can't see why you won't trust them."

"Not now, Eric." his grandfather returned. "I'm busy with this fish."

Eric looked back at the wand in his hand. He lifted it to his right temple. As abruptly as before, everything changed. In the final moments of transition Eric heard fading echoes of his grandfather's words, "Not now, Eric. I'm busy with this fish...busy with this fish...this fish..."

His hand dropped. Eric still stooped onboard the crashed spacecraft. He panned a conclusive look at its interior, before stepping out of the breech.

Immediately his headset COMM link came to life, with Galadriel's artificially worried voice; "Rover 01 now out of VM Base transmission range in excess of standard caution limits. Communication must resume or a search will soon take place. VM Base has already implemented automatic alert measures.

Repeating - VM Mars Rover 01 now out of VM Base transmission range in excess..."

"Damn!" Eric said to his helmet, as he trotted to the rover. "Galadriel, open the rover hatch, and prepare for a return journey to VM Base, right away."

He entered the rover. As he prepared to secure the inner latch, Eric noticed he still held the Grey tool in his gloved hand. Laying it on the edge of the rover's control panel, he secured the latch, and started pressurization.

Chapter 5:
Instantly, Eric's Reality Shattered

The AI computer's artificial voice spoke her standard phrases about pressurization.

But rather than stand by, Eric sat and continued giving commands through helmet COMM link, "Galadriel, plot the shortest course back to VM Base."

Eric's eyes drifted to the wand. What should he do with it?

"Pressurization of VM Mars Rover 01 is complete, Eric. Your environment suit may be removed at this time." Galadriel informed him.

Quickly, Eric went through the steps to remove his helmet, and arm components. Once more he stopped with them.

Eric inquired, "Have you plotted that course?"

Galadriel responded, "Course plotted."

"Refresh the topographic map used earlier and show the plotted course back to VM Base, Galadriel," He impatiently instructed.

The map renewed. Satisfied after looking it over briefly, Eric pulled on his seat strap, and ordered, "Okay, Galadriel initiate course."

Exactly as the rover crested the crater's lip Galadriel's COMM link activated.

The colonel yelled, "...Eric, where the Hell are you? Report! Ensign Eric Sheffield, please report now. I repeat, this is Valles Marineris Base calling Ensign Eric Sheffield, please report now..."

Eric frowned and said, "Okay Galadriel, open a COMM window on the primary screen."

While the largest portion of the screen remained a forward Martian vista, the lower left quadrant turned into a view of Colonel Allen Tillman, at VM Base COMM Center.

As if by instinct, Eric covered the Zeta Reticulan tool with his right hand. It didn't matter, since the colonel failed to notice.

"Ensign Eric Sheffield, reporting, Sir," he said begrudgingly.

"Ensign, where were you?" the Colonel inquired. "We were about to send out a search party, damn it!"

"Sorry Colonel", Eric responded. "I temporarily maneuvered the rover into a crater that cut off communications. I'm now on my way back to VM Base."

"Good, report to me at the botanical lab as soon as you arrive. One of those damn hydroponics units is malfunctioning again, we need your expertise," the annoyed Colonel ordered.

"Aye, Colonel," he replied. "I'll be there straight away."

A look of disgust flooded Colonel Tillman's face as he added, "All right Ensign, just get your ass here as quick as you can; Tillman out."

The COMM window blinked off. Eric relaxed, and released a heavy sigh. He wondered why the Colonel considered it necessary to always be so hard on him. He didn't treat the other crewmembers as harshly.

Eric noted the chronometer display showing time spent, and an estimate of time remaining for the trip back to VM Base. It informed him this journey would take in hours, minutes, and seconds, 2:10:24 and counting down.

Growing boredom crept into Eric's psyche. To fill it, his mind drifted back to recent memories; memories of the trip from L2 Station to Mars. Break-time led him to his favorite view port. Mary Kinsey stood next to it. Out this portal the central vessel, "Marco Polo", and two of the three trinary landing vessels could be seen tumbling through space, spinning on their central axis, creating approximately a third G, while they traveled. This continuous tumbling, made it possible to artificially simulating gravity near Mars normal. By the time they reached their destination all would be acclimated to the feel of Martian gravity. Eric approached Mary and the portal, taking the opportunity for conversation.

"It's a beautiful view isn't it?" he asked with a slight stammer in his voice. Mary made him nervous. She was lovely, but Eric could never hope to compete with Major Hastings.

She glanced at Eric with overt disinterest. Turning back to the portal view, she spat in a decidedly unfriendly tone, "If you say so."

Intimidated into complete silence, Eric fidgeted awkwardly.

Mary continued, "The beauty of the view wasn't on my mind. But you're probably thinking that's all I'd appreciate about it. Typical man; always thinking with your little head, not your big head. Only in your case they're both little!"

Mary walked away, leaving Eric with mouth agape. He turned to stare blankly into space, as a profound sadness gripped his heart. Oblivious to his pain, the trinary sail ships tumbled through space dancing with a vista of stars. Imposed over that view, Eric saw his own reflection. A tear rolled down his cheek. He quickly brushed it away, and tried to put the incident out of his mind. He had little success. The bitter memory still twisted his gut, even as he brought his thoughts back to the present moment.

The Grey wand reentered his mind. He picked it up, and again examined it. As before, he could find no marks on its silvery metallic surface. Based on the hallucination Eric had experienced on the crashed spacecraft, he reasoned this "wand" must be a mind control device. Eric had heard rumors the Zeta Reticulans may have once used devices like this to control unwitting abductees on Earth. Of course, the Greys denied these rumors.

If he hoped to better understand this tool, he must do more experiments. Quick to act on his thoughts, Eric lifted and pointed it at his right temple.

Instantly, Eric's reality shattered. In its place fragments of memories jumbled together into a surreal blend. Like his first use of the wand, Eric's hallucination returned him to his boyhood. This time he was twelve, on the front pew at the funeral home of his grandfather's parting. Eric looked quickly about the room. Everything appeared exactly as he remembered that day. The actual funeral had not yet started. The family took a final private viewing just prior to the event.

The doors burst open. Eric's Great Aunt Sarah came wailing into the room. Following close behind, Great Uncle Jim calmly carried his mini-cam, tripod and other recording equipment.

Aunt Sarah busied herself giving Uncle Jim instructions, "Now, let's try here. Jim, honey, set up the tripod and we'll get some test shots. We want the angle just right for the funeral."

Eric found their behavior difficult to understand. Their ways lacked dignity. He couldn't help but see them as crude people. He felt fortunate that they were not the next in line to be his legal guardians. With both of his parents dead, and then his grandfather gone, his mother's sister, Thelma stood next. She'd just lost her husband, Harlon, his uncle, earlier that year, during the great calamity, just a few weeks before the big disclosure reveal of the alien Greys. As the family called it, Harlon just up and disappear. Grandpa said the Greys took him. Thelma said she thought he was still alive, but where he went and why, she never felt sure. She already had two sons to take care of, but their house had the most room, so that's where the family decided to stick Erlc. He found it all such a depressing state of affairs.

Without thinking, he let those feelings spill from his lips, "Why do they act that way?"

From his left an unexpected answer flared, "Because they're grieving, you ass! What about you; aren't you feeling any grief?"

Eric turned to find Colonel Tillman sitting next to him.

Confused he said, "Naturally I feel grief. And what are you doing here? My Aunt Thelma was sitting next to me, back then. She's the one who taught me that people grieve in their own ways."

With a frown, the Colonel said, "I'm here because some sick piece of your unraveling mind decided I was needed. So, if I have to fill in for your Aunt Thelma, I guess that's what I'm doing here. Why don't you show your grief?"

Eric pondered, and replied much as he had with his Aunt Thelma years before, "Grandfather taught me the importance of always keeping my composure under control. It made him angry when I let my emotions show. He helped me see how it's beneath my dignity to act like them."

Eric remembered how surprised he'd been, when his Aunt Thelma had said in return, "Dad always was a hard one. Don't worry, Eric, Honey, when you live with our family, it'll be alright to express yourself. Around our place, it'd be hard not to."

But in this hallucinatory recreation, for some unknown reason, Aunt Thelma wasn't there. Her caring heart failed to give Eric any comfort, as instead the colonel laughed uncontrollably, pointing at Eric all the while. Other family members joined in the laughter, all pointing at Eric in turn. Uncle Jim turned the mini-cam on Eric. Eric's grandfather sat up in his coffin, lifted his stiff arm, pointed, and joining the macabre laughter. Curtains behind his coffin parted to reveal four Zeta Reticulans all pointing and laughing. The parlor doors opened and hundreds of people flooded into the room all pointing and laughing. One of the laughing Zeta Reticulans held the wand in Eric's direction. As the crowd pressed in, all four little Greys led the rest. Eric's grandfather leapt from his coffin, joining the crowd just behind the Greys. Eric didn't know what to do. The complete madness of the laughing pressing crowd loosened Eric's slippery grip on his own failing sanity. The crowd pressed the Grey pointing the wand within reach.

Abruptly, Eric grabbed the wand form the Grey's gangling hand, and desperately pointed it to his own temple once more. As brusquely as it had begun the nightmare ended.

Eric lowered his arm and stared with disbelief as he saw VM Base on the forward view screen, less than a kilometer ahead.

Chapter 6:
Colonel, Are You Alright?

A panicked thought entered Eric's mind. He realized his find couldn't be kept a secret if anyone else saw the rover's recording of events at the crater. Quickly Eric searched though older recordings from earlier explorations. He found a segment with similar surroundings, and altered that day's recording to eliminate everything about the dune, and its crashed alien contents. He completed this task as the rover came to a stop just inside the rover hanger.

Rover 02, the Bradbury was out.

Rover 03, known as Merlin, sat in its usual parked position. Its constant state of disrepair made it rarely used. The sand sifter never worked quit right on Merlin, but Eric couldn't find the fault. Every time he looked at it, it reminded him of his failure. That day, it didn't matter so much.

Nothing else could come close to the opportunity of studying this incredible alien technology. For a moment he wondered why he had taken such drastic measures to keep it secret. But he knew if the others learned of his mind control tool, they would take it away. Eric couldn't allow that to happen.

Before exiting the rover, Eric opened his environment suit and slipped the wand into his jumper's left breast pocket.

After sealing the environment suit and rover de-pressurization, he debarked the rover hanger. Eric headed straight for the botanical lab, as ordered.

The botanical lab stood out in contrast to the Martian landscape, a geodesic Qantas hut, with triple reinforced semitransparent aluminum sheets stretched over the superstructure. There the Colonel, also a botanist, experimented with various Earth plants grown in Martian soil. In addition to these soil experiments, the colonel also conducted in this same lab hydroponics studies with water extracted from Martian ice.

From the beginning of their mission, the stability monitors for two of the hydroponics units regularly malfunctioned. He'd tried to fix them so many times. Eric knew this maintenance nightmare awaited him at the lab, that and a grumpy colonel. He dreaded both.

As he entered the air lock, Eric reported his presence to Colonel Tillman. After full pressurization, he removed his environment suit, hung it up, and opened the inner door. Across the room, the Colonel pruned a plant. The hollow echo of Eric's footsteps bounced about the lab as he traversed the room.

Without looking around, Colonel Tillman yelled, "Hydroponics unit E2. Get your lazy butt on it right now! I want that stability monitor working within the hour."

Eric went right to that unit. After opening his tool kit, he retrieved the remote control used to direct maintenance robots of the SIDNE series. SIDNE, standing for **S**ynthetic **I**ntelligent **D**iagnostic **N**eurologic **E**ntity, was pronounced like the name Sidney. These small robots were especially useful for diagnostic maintenance of any electronic equipment at VM Base. Like all computer systems on the base, their processors employed artificial intelligence programming and circuitry, synthetically mimicking human neurons. Maintenance Robot - SIDNE 22 responded to Eric's summons, rolling up while announcing his approach with several low beeping tones. Eric could clearly see its model name and number labeled along the side of its tope chaise.

After scanning the surroundings with infrared detectors, SIDNE 22 used a male artificial voice to say, "You called, Eric?"

"That's correct, SIDNE 22," Eric replied. "I need your help diagnosing hydroponics unit E2. Take position behind the unit and remove its outer casing. Attach a circuit reader probe to the primary line, and we'll see what's amiss."

As SIDNE 22 carried out these tasks, Eric glanced at the colonel. It was obvious from Colonel Tillman's tense body language that he remained seriously annoyed.

SIDNE 22 informed, "Ready. Are there further instructions, Eric?"

Eric responded, "Yes, I want you to run a complete diagnostic of the primary internal stability monitoring circuitry."

After an appropriate amount of time, the little robot said, "All circuits scan as ... reliable."

Eric said, "Alright 22, check the secondary internal stability monitoring circuitry."

There was again a brief pause while the small robot carried out the diagnostic. It said, "All circuits scan as ... reliable."

Eric responded, "Okay, SIDNE 22 let's do an analysis of the internal communications bus."

The little robot detached its diagnostic probe and reattached it to a different element of the unit's interior. Several small lights blinked on and off, and a variety of beeps and whirs emitted from SIDNE 22. Upon completion, 22 said, "The internal communications bus scans as ... reliable."

An hour later Eric and SIDNE 22 still worked on the hydroponics unit. As usual, the problem left Eric baffled by the fact that he could find nothing wrong with any part of the unit. It just didn't add up. Unit E2 remained yet another malfunctioning device he couldn't explain. The actual reason was of a nature beyond his imagining. Yet of all the colonists on Mars, he possessed the one clue that could answer this riddle; that vague sensation of being watched. Instinctively he felt the Martian presence, but had no idea of their abilities to telekinetically influence objects at great distances. Eric had no reason to suspect the watchers could possibly be the cause of these inexplicable malfunctions.

The Colonel stepped up behind. "Well", he said.

Stumbling over his words, Eric tried to explain; "Colonel there just isn't anything wrong with it. I've taken it completely apart, and back together again.

SIDNE 22 and I have diagnosed every part, and they are in top-notch shape. All of these parts are assembled exactly according to textbook specs. Theoretically this unit should not be exhibiting any malfunctions. I can't explain it, Sir".

Colonel Tillman left no doubt of his unhappy state of mind, when he said, "I've heard you say that before, Ensign, but then an hour later all of the damn unit's alarms go off. Damn it, Eric find the problem! I don't want to hear any more excuses. Just fix the fucking thing!"

The Colonel turned his back to Eric, prepared to walk away.

"But Sir", Eric pleaded, "are you sure it's not another one of Major Hastings practical jokes?" Eric paused, laughed nervously and added, "He could've programmed a timer setting the alarms off at any designated time, and then buried the program in one of the monitor's regular subroutines. Sir, the point is someone must be, like doing this intentionally. There are no defects in the device."

The Colonel's fury flared. He screamed, "Didn't I tell you I don't want to hear excuses! I'm not convinced anyone on this base has committed the kind of sabotage you're suggesting. And I might add it's unbecoming for you to accuse a superior officer. Now, I suggest you take that unit apart again, and diagnose each part at least three more times."

Eric's jaw dropped, amazed at the arrogant stupidity of the man.

"Don't just stand there with your mouth opened! Get back to work", the colonel yelled.

"Yes Sir", Eric said with a slight tone of distaste.

"Insufferable insubordinate son of a bitch", the Colonel muttered as he turned again to walk back to his pruning.

Something deep inside Eric suddenly snapped. With a continuous swift move, he pulled the wand from his pocket, and quickly pointed it at the back of Colonel Tillman's head. The Colonel stopped and slightly swayed.

Eric lowered the wand, and said, "Colonel, are you alright?"

The Colonel held his forehead, and bowed his head to one side. He slowly turned back toward Eric, reaching for a chair nearby. Eric helped the Colonel into the chair. Still angry, he took the opportunity again and pointed the wand at the back of Colonel Tillman's head.

Holding it there, Eric said, "You think I should give up on the hydroponics unit for now, don't you, Colonel?"

The Colonel appeared in a trance. Dazed he said, "Yes ... I think so."

"I thought you would", Eric said. "You also think, I've done an excellent job, and deserve some extra break time, starting immediately, don't you? Isn't that right, Colonel?"

"Yes ... that's absolutely right," the hollow voiced Colonel Tillman replied.

"That's what I thought. Thank you, Colonel Tillman. I'll look at that unit again tomorrow, unless you think I should just forget it." Eric said, his confidence growing.

The spiritless voice of Colonel Tillman said, "You're probably right ... you should just forget it."

"Thank you, Colonel," Eric said. "I'll be going now. But before I go, I'd like to suggest if any hydroponics monitor alarms sound, it will be as if you cannot hear it. Do you understand, Colonel? You will not hear any hydroponics monitor alarms."

The Colonel flinched, "I understand. I will not hear any hydroponics monitor alarms."

Eric smiled. He slowly moved the wand away, and slipped it back into his pocket.

The Colonel groaned. He lowered his head into his hands, and said, "I have the most incredible headache."

"I'm sorry to hear that, Colonel", said Eric. "Is there anything I can do to help?"

The Colonel's great pain quite apparent, he said, "No, Eric ... you go ahead. Take a break. You deserve extra time off, now."

A smug grin grew onto Eric's lips. He nodded and said, "Thanks again, Colonel. I hope your headache ends soon."

Chapter 7:
They've Got Their Reasons

Eric stepped into the botanical lab's airlock. Once back in his environment suit, he walked to the VM Base Prime Facility. The base medical rooms, communication center, and crew quarters were all housed within this prime facility, also designed as the eventual launch capsule. When their assignment period ended, this prime capsule would eventually take off, leaving behind the remainder of the base structures after additional and replacement crews arrived in approximately two Earth years.

After boarding the Prime Facility, and striping off his suit, Eric headed for his sleep chamber. He pulled the curtain, which gave his chamber a modicum of privacy. He released a heavy sigh of relief, glad to finally be alone.

Eric reached into his jumper pocked and retrieved the wand. The thought passed through his mind, he probably shouldn't do anything more with it. In spite of these thoughts, he pointed the wand at his temple. As before, his reality changed.

Eric lay on an operating table. With the exception of his head, which he could turn side to side slightly, his body seemed otherwise quite immobile. Several Zeta Reticulans stood around the table. Their dark piercing eyes drilled into his soul. Eric looked down at himself. He was naked, and again an adolescent. He could feel the long spindly fingers of the Greys touching him in different places.

"What are you doing to me?" he cried out.

The Zeta Reticulans backed up until they were outside Eric's line of sight. He turned his head to the left. Another operating table sat next to his, with Eric's grandfather stretched out. He appeared asleep.

Eric yelled, "Grandfather, wake up!"

The old man's eyes fluttered opened. He faced Eric, and said, "Eric, I told you we could never trust the Greys." His voice wavered, as he added, "Now you can see why."

"But grandfather, what's happening? Why are they doing this?" Eric asked.

"They've got their reasons. Who can say what they are?" replied Eric's grandfather. He turned his head to face the ceiling, and said, "I told you not to play wIth that Grey tool, didn't I? Yet you persisted; just like your mother, and your aunt Thelma always so head strong. They were quite the inseparable pair when they were your age."

Many Zeta Reticulans gathered around Eric's grandfather. Their hands and arms moved quickly, but with several of them between Eric and his grandfather, blocking his view, Eric could not make out their actions. Sounds of the rending of human flesh and bones breaking, could be heard. Eric's grandfather cried out in agony.

"Stop it!" Eric yelled. "Leave him alone. He never did anything to you; Stop!"

One Zeta Reticulan approached Eric's table. In his hand Eric saw the wand. With it, the Grey touched Eric's temple. In his mind Eric heard words of comfort; "Fear not; it is for the best. It doesn't really harm him. He will not remember."

The other Zeta Reticulans parted from around Eric's grandfather. His grandfather's hair was gone. His head made much larger, Eric's grandfather appeared like a cross between himself and a Zeta Reticulan. He looked as though they had transformed him into some sort of hybrid.

Fear and revulsion grabbed hold of Eric. He cried, "Grandfather, what have they done to you?"

Calmly Eric's grandfather turned his bulbous head to face Eric, saying, "Fear not; it's for the best. One by one, we will all be replaced, like some of your crewmates already have."

"No!" Eric screamed. "It can't be!"

Suddenly Eric could move. He jumped from the table, punched the nearest Zeta Reticulan and grabbed the wand simultaneously. The Zeta Reticulan squealed like a small wounded animal. It fell limp on the floor.

In an instant the Grey transformed into his mummified counterpart, like those Eric had seen on the crashed ship. Confused, Eric turned to look again at his grandfather, seeking understanding. He didn't find what he sought. His half grandfather, half Zeta Reticulan withered before his eyes into a mummy, as well. All the other Zeta Reticulans, also mummified, came toward Eric, like nightmare alien zombies. Eric backed up from their approach. He looked down at his hand to see he still held the wand. Desperately, he touched it to his temple.

In an instant, his awareness returned to his sleeping chamber. All returned to normal; or had it? Things felt somehow different. Eric lay awake, unable to rest his mind. This latest nightmare vision haunted his meditations, relentlessly. After lying there long enough to know he wouldn't be able to sleep, he decided to seek out help. Eric made his way to the medical bay. He hoped Dr. La Claire might be there, and maybe give him something to make sleep easier.

Eric entered the med bay doorway. He saw the doctor studying a monitor showing an electron microscope image, of something cellular or some such thing. It didn't really interest Eric.

Dr. Beatrice La Claire briefly glanced from her work at Eric. The expected frown crept onto her lips.

Gazing back at her monitor, she said, "What can I do for you, Eric?"

Eric replied, "Doc. I've been having trouble sleeping. Do you think you could give me a little something to counter this insomnia?"

Dr. La Claire arose. Grasping a diagnostic light, she pointed to a medical table, and said, "sit."

Eric sat.

Using her examination light, the doctor studied Eric's, ears. She then carried out the traditional open wide and say awe routine, followed by checking his eyes. The pupils of Eric's eyes contracted dramatically. He found the bright light very disorienting.

Dr. La Claire suggested, "Eric I want you to lie back and place your head into that small cushioned brace at the head of the examination table."

"Now Eric", she further instructed, "you must lay perfectly still for a few seconds while I check your head with this handheld portable magnetic resonance scanner."

The doctor passed the scanner over Eric's head. He felt the vibrations of its gentle thumping.

Eric's focus remained blurred. His eyes resisted recovery from Doctor La Claire's bright examination light. For a brief moment Dr. La Claire looked different. Her head had somehow grown much larger, shaped like a giant upside down pear. The doctor's skin became pale chalky grey, and her eyes were dark, enlarged, and slightly slanted. A rush of panic went through Eric as he remembered his grandfather's warning, *"One by one, we will all be replaced, as some of your crewmates have already."*

"No!" Eric screamed, as he sat up. "It can't be!"

"Calm yourself, Ensign", Dr. La Claire said, with growing caution.

Eric regained his composure, as he looked back at the doctor and saw her appearance returned to normal. He panted and signed, and knew that he must be thoroughly confusing the doctor, with his erratic behavior. Eric reached up to rub his forehead.

Looking down at the floor, with trembling voice, he said, "I'm sorry Doctor, my nerves are a little on edge, and I really need something to help me sleep."

A tingle of fear momentarily entered the doctor's mind. Nervously, she reached for a hypo-sprayer complete with sedative ready for use.

"This should help you rest", she said as she prepared his arm for the hypo-sprayer.

Dr. La Claire checked the pressure gages, making sure the hypo-sprayer had sufficient pressure for use.

Eric's eyes converged on the highly reflective metallic surface of the hypo-sprayer's casing. He noticed her hands quivering slightly. This in turn caused strange forms to play in the shiny casing's reflections. Eric blinked, as suddenly, within these reflections the doctor's semblance appeared to once again transform into the bizarre Zeta/Human hybrid.

Eric panicked. He could not allow this replacement of the doctor to use the hypo-sprayer on him. She would replace him while he slept sedated. Eric quickly retrieved the wand from his jumper pocket, leapt from the examination table, and pointed it directly at the doctor's temple. Griped by an invisible force, the doctor jerked into an uncanny zombie-like state. Her stance became unstable, as she swayed. Eric smiled.

"Now, Doctor", He said, "you want to hand me that hypo-sprayer; don't you?"

Moving slowly still swaying, the doctor extended the hypo-sprayer, and said, "I want to hand you this hypo-sprayer; don't I?"

Eric took the hypo. Like the doctor before, he checked the gages, and observed the hypo-sprayer fully pressurized, and ready to deliver 10 ccs of the sedative within. He also noted the drug canister attached to it contained a total of 80 ccs.

With unceremonious abruptness Eric used the hypo-sprayer on Dr. La Claire. He helped her to her workstation chair, designed to recline, with securing straps for landing and launching. Eric instructed the doctor to quickly strap herself in. By the time she pulled the last strap in place, her hands slipped, showing clear signs of the sedative taking effect. Eric looked back at the hypo-sprayer gages. It contained 70 ccs, with the pressure built-up for another dose. Eric reasoned since the doctor's replacement wasn't really human, it might take more than one human dose to thoroughly sedate her.

He administered a second 10 ccs directly to her throat. Soon thereafter, she was massively unconscious. Eric lifted the wand from Dr. La Claire's head, and pocketed it. He leaned into her closely.

Her breathing grew shallow.

He wondered, 'Might she need another?'

So Eric gave her a third spay, and once the pressure built up again, a forth.

'That should be enough to finish her off,' He thought in passing. As it turned out, he framed that thought more correctly than he consciously realized.

Eric stepped away from the slowly expiring doctor, while remembering that his grandfather's words of warning had been plural; *"crewmates"*, not just crewmate. Eric reasoned there must be more replaced hybrids on the base. He must purge the base of all such alien infiltrations, before they could manage to replace the entire crew. This had become his righteous mission.

To defeat these invaders, Eric decided on a strategy of doing the unexpected. He must launch the prime facility. They would never anticipate such a move. After launching he could pilot the capsule to the *"Marco Polo"*, still in orbit. Since the extensive damage to a third of its solar wind sails made it irreparable, this had forced the *Marco Polo* to remain in orbit and become a new Martian orbital station. The Tellurian Space Agency sent additional supplies from Earth, with more planned to arrive soon, and the station had, by that time, become quite well established.

Eric still vividly remembered the day their solar sail ripped out of control. He stood gazing out his favorite view port at the growing yet still diminutive rusty Martian ball. He stared intently as that red world, slowly approached.

Suddenly clouds of micrometeorites pelted their vessel. From his vantage point, Eric watched in horror as the weakened portion of the sail escalated into a massive tear. Abruptly, his day went from exciting exploration to cataclysmic chaos. Everything was thrown, when the rotation pattern that created their artificial Mars-like gravity fell out of sync. Eric still marveled at how well and how quickly the Marco Polo's captain managed to get things back under control.

Thinking fast the captain ordered their sails completely unfurled, until they cleared the clouds of micrometeorites. This saved the other two sails from damage. However, once they later redeployed those saved sails, their progress continued on but greatly slowed.

Five long and fitful months later the Marco Polo hobbled into orbit. EVA repair crews did what they could with the torn sail, but due to extensive damage, *Marco Polo* could not make the return journey back to the Earth system. Instead it remained in orbit of Mars, converted into the space station Eric then pinned his hopes on as the best bet for their survival. He took false comfort in the idea he could get help with the alien infiltration there, until further backups came from Earth.

But, before he could launch the VM prime capsule, he must be sure about all of their crewmembers' whereabouts. Eric had to learn who among the crew had been co-opted, and who could still be trusted, or at least controlled with the wand. With the help of the wand, he reasoned, he could save VM Base from this alien threat.

He laughed nervously at the irony of using this alien device as a way to eliminate the attack of these alien hybrids.

With little more thought, an idea came to him. The remote sensor array, controlled from the flight deck, became his next destination. With the array, he could locate all seven crewmembers, no matter where they might be within the entire Valles Marineris Base Prime Facility.

Chapter 8:
And Replace It

As Eric entered the flight deck, he found Major Hastings already there. In his right hand Eric held the wand, and in his left hand he still grasped the hypo-sprayer.

Major Hastings turned briefly from looking at a computer console to say, "Good, Eric, I can use your help." He continued, as he turned back to viewing the console, "I have disengaged fuel tank three for standard maintenance and hose replacement. I think we may have a small leak from one of the hoses connecting fuel tank three to the prime facility's launching thrusters. I want you to suit up and check all exterior hoses, while I monitor your progress from here. Together, we can isolate the bad hose, and replace it."

Something struck Eric as strange about the way Hastings said the words, "and replace it." Eric puzzled, then it occurred to him. Hastings has already been replaced, just like the doctor. And now the Hastings replacement plotted to keep Eric from launching the prime capsule. That must be the real reason this false Hastings disengaged fuel tank three. These hybrids were clearly smarter than he first thought. They anticipated his plan. There couldn't really be anything wrong with the fuel hoses, Eric concluded.

Of course, Eric had no way of knowing the hose problem actually did exist, exactly as Major Hastings described. Like so many malfunctions plaguing their base, the subsurface Myripods caused it telekinetically. To the Martians it simply meant another way to distract the Earth invaders, keeping them busy, preventing discovery of the Myripods' underground world.

Convinced the major co-opted by the enemy, Eric advanced toward Major Hastings, and extended the wand into position to take control of him. Hastings caught a peripheral glimpse of Eric's movements.

He swiveled the chair around to face Eric, and deflected the wand from his head with his left arm. A struggle ensued between the two men.

Next Eric tried to use the hypo-sprayer to actually hit Hastings, but the Major effectively countered that attack with a swift martial-arts kick, which sent Eric sprawling backward to the floor. Eric lost his grip on the wand when he fell. It slid across the floor toward the hatchway of the flight deck.

As he jumped on Eric to pin him down, Hastings yelled, "Eric, what the Hell's wrong with you? Have you gone mad?"

"No", Eric screamed, "just the reverse!"

With that Eric managed to free his left arm. He still held the hypo-sprayer in his left hand. Before Hastings could stop him, Eric hypo injected 10 c.c.s into Hastings' shoulder.

Hastings fumbled to get the hypo-sprayer from Eric. In doing so Eric was able to pull his right arm from the pin. He punched Hastings with a right cross to the jaw.

Hastings fell to the floor. Then on his back, the sedative coursing through his veins, his consciousness threatened to ebb. He tried to fight off the growing sluggish effects and staggered to an almost standing position.

The pressure was back up on the hypo-sprayer. Eric used it again on the weakening Major Hastings, this time applying it directly to the jugular vein.

Hastings slumped to the floor, unable to continue the struggle.

Eric stood over his victim, looking down with a smile of satisfaction at a job well done. What he saw, was a Zeta/Human hybrid Hastings slightly flinching from the internal conflict between the sedative and the need to remain awake. This flinching convinced Eric of the necessity for a third hypo-spray injection. Then like with the doctor, Eric decided that four doses should complete the job.

After delivering the fourth dose to Major Hastings, he'd emptied the hypo-sprayer. Eric slipped it into one of the many pockets of his jump suit. It might be handy later, if he managed to get another canister of the sedative.

He looked about the flight deck, to find the wand near the hatchway. After retrieving it, Eric gazed back at Major Hastings, slumped in a heap on the floor.

Eric positioned himself behind Hastings and hoisted his body up, grasping under each arm. He pulled the Major's body to the copilot's chair and managed to situate him into a proper upright position and strapped him in, as if prepared for launching. Upon completion of this task, Eric slumped into the pilot's chair next to Hastings, exhaling a sigh of fatigue.

Eric sat, contemplating his next move, when Lt. Lou Whey, the navigator, and exobiology expert of the VM base crew, stepped into the hatchway to the flight deck.

"Eric", he said, with an expression of confusion, "What was all that raucous about?"

Only then Eric realized his struggle with Major Hastings had attracted attention. He frowned, unsure about just what to do. Whey stood too far out of reach for the wand. And he didn't want to risk further attention with another struggling skirmish. He sat looking rather dumb founded; as he saw Lt. Whey's eyes begin to survey the rooms contents. His stare came to rest upon Major Hastings.

"Major Hastings!" Exclaimed Lt. Whey. "Eric, what has happened?"

At that point, Lt. Whey made the wrong move. He entered the flight deck, going to Hastings' side.

Eric seized the opportunity and quickly moved the wand into position. With the wand's help, he grappled Lt. Whey's mind into submission. Eric took control.

He said, "Lt. Whey, VM base is under attack. Alien parasites have taken control of both the Doctor, and Major Hastings. They have each been sedated for their safety, and ours. You are to contact the Colonel, and inform him of the need to launch the prime facility. We must evacuate VM Base before this alien infection spreads to all of us. After launching, we are to rendezvous with the *Marco Polo* in orbit. The Colonel will pilot the craft; you will navigate. These orders come directly from Tellurian Space Central Control."

Under the hypnotic guidance of the wand, Lt. Whey believed all of Eric's story as if they were known facts.

Eric slowly moved the wand away from Lt. Whey's head, and backed toward the hatchway of the flight deck.

Lt. Whey immediately sat behind the navigation control panel. He looked back at Eric, and said, "Oh good, Eric, you're still here. I need you to suit up and go to the far side of the rover shed. Lt. Murphy and a pod of maintenance robots are about 800 meters northwest of the crater lip, working on the rover I took out yesterday. It broke down where it sits on my way back. Anyway, you need to take another rover to get her, and bring her back for the evacuation launching. Okay, pronto Mr., I have to call the Colonel."

Eric smiled with satisfaction surging throughout his body. He said, "Yes sir, right away, sir."

He turned and exited the hatchway. Eric marveled at how well events had played into his hands. Now that he had learned where to find Lt. Hilda Murphy, he knew the whereabouts of all but one of the VM base crew. Lt. Commander Mary Kinsey, hydro-geologist, and life support specialist remained the last crewmember unaccounted for. Eric thought she might be in her sleep chamber, since he knew it happened to be during her off duty cycle.

He decided it would be a good idea, before suiting up, to check Lt. Commander Kinsey's chamber. He felt compelled to insure her safety.

Eric found the curtain drawn, an indication of her likely presence, with a desire to be left alone, possibly sleeping.

With wand in hand, Eric approached Mary's chamber cautiously. His nerves on edge, he reached for the curtain. From the beginning of the mission Eric had found Mary very attractive. Yet she'd always been distant and unapproachable. Eric tried his best to keep his attraction a secret from her, since he knew only too well that Mary did not share these feelings in any kind of mutual fashion. In spite of this, he recognized that she detected, and resented his feelings. This explained her cruelty to him throughout their mission. But now things were different. The wand in his hand afforded him an opportunity he dared not allow to form into a complete thought. Yet, he could scarcely pass up such an opportunity. Without the wand, he knew she'd never respond positively, she would in fact no doubt speak to him cruelly as she so often had before. But with the wand, he could shape the thoughts and feelings of others. The temptation grabbed hold of him and became more than his self-constraint could withstand.

Eric quickly thrust the curtain opened, before he had a change of heart. Until that moment Mary slept. She awoke, with a start. She managed to do nothing more than gasp, before Eric had the wand pointed to her temple.

"I've always wanted you, Mary," Eric said, "and you've always wanted me too, haven't you?"

Under any other circumstances she would have not agreed, but Eric knew that this time she could not deny him. Eric smiled, as his expectations grew fulfilled.

He continued to clutch the wand in place next to Mary's head. Eric instructed, Now, Mary you want to unzip the front of my jumper, don't you?

Mary dropped the sheet she had initially held up to her neck. This revealed her ample breasts, which bounced lightly as she reached up to pull Eric's zipper down. Her hand paused at the bottom of the zipper briefly. She parted the jumpsuit and reached into the crouch bringing forth Eric's ample manhood already mostly erect.

He moaned with the mere pleasure of Mary's touch. Then before he could give her any further instructions, he felt the wonder of her lips sliding down the length of his penis. Excitedly Eric thrust against Mary's downward stroke, and began to pump. For a moment Eric almost lost his grip on the wand, and panicked at the thought of what would happen if he dared to take the wand away from Mary's head.

Involuntarily, his erection started to slack off a little.

He decided to not experiment with such a dangerous thing. Eric relaxed his mind, and soon regained his confidence and full erection.

He told Mary to lie back slowly. As she did, he carefully kept the wand pointing at her temple, and penetrated her as he leaned forward over her. Like a ravenous beast he had his way with her, as she writhed with hypnotically simulated ecstasy.

When he finished with her, Eric used the wand to put Mary back to sleep, telling her, "You'll see our sexual encounter as a dream, a pleasant dream, one you'll now think of as a dream to be fulfilled. Dream on so sweetly, Mary, Love."

Mary returned to sleep.

Eric sat next to her, gazing at her face. She looked strangely peaceful, considering what he'd just done to her.

Eric shifted his gaze from Mary to the wand still in his hands. He toyed with it, absent-mindedly, trying to hold back feelings of guilt. It was true that he had wanted her as long as he had known her, but not this way.

Chapter 9:
Warning, Depressurization Eminent!

Very deliberately, he pointed the wand at his own temple once more. Eric did this, almost as if to punish himself for the violation he had just carried out with Mary. But he knew deep down inside there could be no sufficient punishment he might choose to inflict upon himself that could ever be strong enough to truly pay for the indignity of what he'd just done to Mary.

The wand activated; reality shifted into a broken state...

Eric returned to another scenario as a teenager again, back on board a Zeta Reticulan spacecraft. He laid naked and paralyzed on one of their examination tables.

Four Greys gathered around him. One of them held an odd looking cylindrically shaped object attached to a hose like tube, extending off to the right out of Eric's field of vision. The tip of the object consisted of several metallic tentacles. At first they all extend outward straight and stiff from the tip of the hose.

Once activated, these tentacles flared out, separating from each other, while setting into a whirling continuous wiggling motion. It made visceral buzzing and whirring sounds that reminded Eric of a dentist drill.

Two of the Zeta Reticulans lifted Eric's legs and strapped them to supports, which held his legs up and apart. The Grey with the tubular device thrust the writhing tentacles into a place, Eric found most unpleasant, at first.

He could feel the metallic tentacles gyrating within his colon. In spite of how much he found it undesirable, he sensed an involuntary erection approaching. He fought it, but the erection grew out of his control.

Abruptly, one of the Zeta Reticulans placed a warm flexible sheath shaped apparatus on his erection.

Eric opened his mouth to yell out a protest, when another of the Greys shoved yet some other tubular object all the way down his throat. It was coated with a bitter lubricate. Though actually rather brief in duration, the experience seemed a vivid tormented eternity.

Eric ejaculated. The flexible sheath device sucked up the entire spasm. Eric writhed in a tormented mixture of both agony, and ecstasy.

Suddenly, he awoke. He looked at Mary again, still sleeping calmly. Eric zipped up his jumpsuit and left her quickly. He headed to his next task, trying to forget all that had just transpired. He failed to achieve such forgetfulness.

As he suited up, to go out to the rover shed, Eric kept seeing Mary's innocent calm sleeping face. No sooner would he banish the vision from his mind, than he would hear the buzzing of the whirling metallic tentacles echoing from some dark corner of his psyche. The bitter oily taste of the throat probe returned as if it intruded his mouth at the moment. Eric tried to ignore these hallucinations, as he slipped the wand in an outer pocket of his environment suit. He didn't know whether or not he might need it to control Hilda, but he figured it might be best to be prepared, just in case.

He tried to concentrate purely on the tasks of the moment as he clamped his helmet down. With the sealing of his suit, Eric could hear a slight rush of air. This sound stimulated his memory of the slurping sheath like device. It all added up to more than he could stand.

Eric flung himself against the air-lock wall. Rocking his helmet back and forth, he whimpered, begging God to make it all go away. As he muttered this desperate prayer, he punched the air release pad to depressurize the air lock.

The computer voice chimed in his helmet speakers; "Depressurization of VM Base air lock 03 has begun. Depressurization will be complete in 3 minutes. Eric, please…" The computer synthesized voice droned on. Eric's numb mind blotted out the sound.

Eric stood against the wall, waiting for the air pressure gage to indicate a level equal to the outside.

He waited.

He prayed.

He wept.

"Depressurization of VM Base air lock 03 is now complete. You may now open the hatch and debark, Eric." the VM Base AI computer informed Eric.

With a slight tremor in his voice, Eric commanded the main base's AI computer, "Open."

Eric turned to view the Martian landscape stretching forth from the air lock door. The sun hovered about half way between noon and sunset. A tiny reflective replica of this Martian sun glistened on a teardrop clinging just under Eric's right eye.

Eric stepped through the air lock door. The miniature solar reflection rolled down his cheek, and landed at the right most corner of his lips. The salty fluid seeped into his mouth. In response, he licked his lips. Somehow the salty taste made the moment more vivid.

He slowly trudged through the well-trod Martian sand toward the rover shed. Many times before this day, Eric had made this trip, yet that afternoon with so much changed inside him, the familiar walking path seemed somehow remote, almost unknown. Just the same, he walked as if by rote directly to the rover shed.

Rovers 01 and 03 remained in their respective stalls, as Eric had left them earlier that day. He went to Rover 01, which at the time, turned out to be the only functional rover of the lot. He decided that since the trip to pick up Hilda would be so short, he wouldn't bother to pressurize the cabin, and just keep his environment suit on, the whole trip. So, Eric channeled computer control commands to Galadriel though his suit's COMM link.

He commanded, "Galadriel, please focus external sensors to the area approximately 800 meters northwest of the crater's lip surrounding Valles Marineris Base. You should be able to easily locate the proximity beacon on Rover 02. Once you've found it, plot and then set a course to rendezvous with Rover 02."

Almost immediately upon finishing his command, the computer responded, "Located. Course plotted. Rover 01 should rendezvous with Rover 02, the Bradbury in approximately 2.45 minutes. Please stand by, Eric."

Before being fully satisfied, Eric commanded, "Oh yeah, and Galadriel, set primary view screen, in forward vista mode, please."

Eric sat blankly staring at the view screen for the short duration of his trip to pick up Hilda. He felt numb by the time the rover reached the crest of the crater's lip.

In the distance he could see the broken down Bradbury. After another half minute he saw Hilda in her environment suit, working with a pod of SIDNE maintenance robots. They worked together on the rover's left front tread, torn almost clean through. All of this Eric viewed in defiance to a haze of bitter tears, tears he couldn't wipe away, since he still wore his environment suit's helmet.

Biting back his morose self-loathing, Eric commanded, "Galadriel, open up a COMM link with Lt. Hilda Murphy, just outside of the Bradbury."

In less than a second the AI computer responded, "COMM link activated."

"Lt. Murphy, this is Ensign Eric Sheffield, on orders from the Colonel. I am to pick you up and take you back to the Prime Capsule for emergency lift off." Eric wondered if his quivering voice betrayed his shaken emotions.

After a moment of static, Eric's COMM speakers came to life with the sound of Hilda's voice.

"That's not a very good joke, Eric!" She said with a tone somewhere between amused, and mildly annoyed.

Eric paused. Out of all the officers stationed at Valles Marineris Base, Hilda had always been the fairest, and the kindest. While, like all of the others, she too out ranked him, unlike the rest of the VM Base crewmembers, she at least treated him with what he saw as proper human respect. She almost always addressed him by his first name, and insisted that he do the same with her, except in the presence of the Colonel, who disapproved of such familiarity.

"No, Hilda," Eric said, his voice clearly wavering, "This is no joke. VM Base has been infiltrated by an alien contamination. Those of us unaffected must evacuate immediately."

Rover 01 slowly came to a stop beside Rover 02. Before Hilda could respond to Eric's last words, Galadriel informed them both through their helmet COMM speakers, "Rover 01 has completed the rendezvous with Rover 02. Actual duration was 2.47 minutes. Are there further orders, Eric?"

Silently Eric stared at the view screen, almost as if afraid to move. Hilda stood looking at Rover 01. Her posture became increasingly impatient.

"Well", Hilda said as she rested her hands upon her hips. Even in her environment suit, the meaning stood out as obvious. "Eric, what's it going to be?

Are you coming out, or am I going to have to come in and get you?"

Shaking lose the cobwebs of his morose lethargy, Eric arose, tripped the securing latch and commanded, "Galadriel open the hatch, please."

As the hinges of the hatch turned, Eric said to Hilda, "You don't know how sorry, I am about all of this."

Eric stepped out of the rover. It was immediately obvious to him, as he had already suspected. He could see right into Hilda's helmet faceplate. She'd clearly already become one of them.

Moving quickly, Eric swung the wand into place. He could see how Hilda tried to fight off the effects.

She strained against the trance, and knocked Eric's arm aside, crying, "Eric what's wrong with you? What are you doing?"

The wand fell on a bed of red Martian sand.

Eric lunged at Hilda, and reached around her environment suit, tearing away the auxiliary re-breather hose.

Putting all of her weight behind it, Hilda shoved Eric away and to the ground. It didn't matter about the difference between Earth and Mars gravity, she still out massed Eric, and came close to matching his muscularity. But before she could accomplish pushing him away, Eric managed to secure a grip on her primary re-breather hose. As Hilda's push threw him backward off his feet, he pulled the hose unfastened, just before losing his grip on it.

He landed on his back, his left shoulder hitting a rock with great force. The pain caused his reality to fade briefly.

Hilda's environment suit internal computer monitoring system activated the auto alert, saying,

"Warning, Depressurization eminent! Warning, Depressurization eminent!"

Eric's awareness returned.

Abruptly, he sat up.

Eric saw Hilda fumbling with her primary re-breather hose, seeking to re-engage it.

'Unfortunately', Eric thought, 'it just looks like she might succeed, unless...'

He picked up the rock he'd just banged his shoulder against and hurled it in her direction. It struck Hilda squarely in the front of her helmet faceplate. The blow caused her to loose footing, and down she went.

Her fumbling stopped. Eric sat, watching, waiting.

The auto alert in Hilda's environment suit paused, then concluded with deadly finality, 'Warning, Depressurization complete."

Eric stood over Hilda's limp body. He stared into her broken helmet faceplate. He wondered what it might be like to end. Her head had not exploded as many popular science fiction stories so often incorrectly depicted. However, blood ruptured from many of her natural body opening.

Eric noticed that after a short time the blood coming from her mouth, nose, ears, and eyes stopped flowing. Much of it formed a pool, in which the back of her head rested. It didn't take long for her hair to become quite thoroughly saturated with her blood.

As he watched, Eric saw the color of her blood slowly change from a bright red to a more brownish red tone. After staring at her for so long, time lost much of its meaning, he came to realize her face no longer looked anything like the alien / human hybrid he had seen earlier.

He turned away from Hilda's corpse. His mind raced with horrifying thoughts. He wondered, 'Could I have been mistaken? Was she really just an innocent human? What have I done?'

He resumed looking into her cold dead bloody eyes, as if seeking an answer to his tormented thoughts. The only answers he found there, gave Eric no comfort.

Chapter 10:
Your Eyes Can Deceive You

The direction of Eric's gaze shifted from Hilda's frozen face to the wand now lying on the ground to her left.

Once again Eric felt compelled to use the wand on himself. He retrieved it and proceeded to point it at the side of his helmet.

It felt as though everything changed, and yet nothing appeared different. He still stood on the sands of Mars, next to Hilda's corpse, and the two rovers, Galadriel and the Bradbury.

Then the sound of many cymbals being struck came from all around. The sound penetrated deeply into his eardrums. This shattering cacophony distressed his ears, like tiny drills boring through them into his brain.

Eric dropped to his knees, pointlessly clasping his hands on the sides of his helmet, as if he could somehow block the agonizing sound out of his aching ears.

As abruptly as it has begun this piercing clamor suddenly ceased.

"It's a fine mess, you've made of things," said the voice of Eric's Grandfather, as if from somewhere behind. "So, you thought you could master that alien tool. Ha, only now you must be starting to realize that instead it masters you."

Eric swiftly stood and turned, awkwardly.

His Grandfather, as a hybrid, stood on the sands of Mars with no environment suit. He wore the formal robes of a Zeta Reticulan ambassador.

Instinctively, Eric stepped backwards, almost tripping on a rock.

"See," Eric's hybridized Grandfather, said tauntingly, "hybrids don't need environment suits on Mars. Ha, you needlessly killed her. You're a miserable failure, you know. Your Colonel Tillman's been right about you all along. You really are a no-count alright!"

"No!" Eric screamed, "Stop it Grandfather! She was a hybrid. I saw it."

"Maybe", Eric's Grandfather leaned closer to him, "You shouldn't always trust what you see. I've told you before that your eyes can deceive you. But did you listen?"

Pointing to the wand in Eric's hand his hybrid Grandfather continued, "Especially when you've been sipping a little too much on that alien hypnotic juice."

Eric jerked the wand away from his Grandfather's pointing hand. In an instant Eric stood alone.

Before he could inhale another breath, his helmet COMM came to life, "Eric, Hilda, what's keeping you two? We need to launch; Over."

Eric glanced at Hilda, on the ground next to his feet. His focus shifted from Hilda's frozen horror struck face to the reflection on her cracked faceplate. There he saw his own tear stained face looking down at her. To his shock and un-reconcilable dismay he saw his own face as a hybrid. He could not deny it. The infection had spread to him. Eric again fell to his knees.

He responded to Lt. Whey, "You'll have to go on without us. They had already gotten to Hilda. And now it looks like I'm infected as well. Hilda's dead, and I'm as good as it. Go on without me. Warn the others. Don't come back here to Valles Marineris. Humans must never return here. This whole place is contaminated with the alien threat; Over."

Lt. Whey returned, "Eric, you're talking crazy. You've got to come back to the base; Over."

Snapping back, Eric said, "I can't come back. Didn't you hear me? I'm infected too, now. You have to leave without me. Your escape has no meaning otherwise. Now go; Over and out."

After a brief pause, Lt. Whey said, "God be with you Eric. Lt. Lou Whey, out."

Eric bowed his head and returned to sobbing. Long a loner, Eric never before felt as alone as in that moment.

It didn't seem many seconds later that the launching engines ignited, and the VM Capsule began its ascent.

Eric looked up from his remorse to see the launch. At least, the few survivors would finally escape this infectious infiltration.

The capsule lifted no more than two meters, when Eric's COMM link came to life with the voice of Lt. Whey as he reported, "We have a red light. Indicators say a fuel leak from tank three!"

Eric rose, while fear locked into his every muscle. 'Could it be?', he thought, taking one tentative step forward, 'Could the replacement of Major Hastings have been telling the truth about that fuel leak? Is the leak real?'

Eric heard Colonel Tillman's voice yelling, "I'm switching to tank four."

Whey again cried out, "It's too late! We're losing pressure on tank three; fast, we'll have to...", his words abruptly cut short by a massive explosion disintegrating the launch capsule before Eric's eyes.

A second explosion consumed the base of the prime facility, from which the capsule lifted. Another moment later the rover shed and hydroponics lab exploded in chain reaction fashion.

When the shock wave reached Eric, he found himself thrown off his feet backwards several meters. His helmet missed hitting a large rock by less than two centimeters. He lay for a moment, recovering his breath.

Eric sat up. He checked his suit for damage. He was lucky, or so he thought.

He stood, and stepped closer to the crater's lip overlooking the smoldering Valles Marineris Base. Since the atmosphere had little oxygen, the base would only burn as long as its fuel and oxygen supply lasted. After that the base would slowly turn cold and dead.

Before Eric could wonder how he'd survive, he saw a most perplexing sight. Through the smoke he could barely see it. Something hovered in the air. He could just make it out at a great distance, just above the horizon beyond the smoldering base. Bewildered, he realized by line of sight, it hovered in the same general direction of the downed Zeta Reticulan craft.

Eric ran back to the rover, not realizing he had dropped the wand when the blast knocked him off his feet. It rested on the ground near where he had stood. A bed of Martian dust became the wand's lonely place of repose, never again to impress twisted visions into Eric's tormented mind.

Chapter 11:
Are There Further Orders, Eric?

Back in the rover, Eric said, "Galadriel I need you to focus your sensors on that hovering object beyond VM Base." After a deep breath, he inquired, "What is it?"

"Analysis of sensor data, confirms this is the same metallic craft earlier recorded under the sand dune at vector coordinates 32.456 by 25.163 by 7.119, relative to VM Base. The object is now moving through the air, maintaining a consistent elevation level relative to the ground."

"Alright Galadriel," Eric returned, "Plot a course to intercept and follow this craft at ground level. If these aliens want to play cat and mouse, I'll go with it."

The rover jerked into motion. Progress seemed slow at first. The course Galadriel plotted took the rover back near the smoldering base.

Looking at the debris, Eric easily concluded there could be no chance of any survivors. Pieces of the shattered base endured only in a thoroughly destroyed state. When the rover finished passing through the scattered remains of the base, Eric immediately put the depressing thoughts of the VM base demise out of his mind, and tried to give his full attention to his current goal; bringing a decisive end to this alien menace.

It soon became apparent that the Zeta Reticulan saucer ship was leading Eric deeper and deeper into the valley. In time the rover followed a path directly parallel to a tall sand shrouded cliff face. Eric had previously looked into this valley from the top of the cliff before, but he'd never been this deep in the valley itself.

The forward sensors indicated that the Grey spacecraft had begun to lower and appeared to be about to land very near the cliff wall. On his front view screen, Eric could just barely see the ship coming down.

"Galadriel", he ordered, "Magnify forward view screen 18 X. Center focus on the alien craft itself and follow its movements."

With amazing abruptness the zoom took effect. Eric could clearly see the craft coming very close to land. But, just about three meters above the ground the ship stopped and established a spin. At first the craft spun slowly, but with each revolution it increasingly gained more momentum. Soon it's speed attained a considerable kick. Sand blew about from the cliff wall, as a result of the fanning effect of the spinning craft.

The magnification of the view screen had become too close for Eric to have a proper perspective of what happened. He commanded, "Galadriel, please reduce magnification to 16 X and continue reducing the X value in increments of 1 for each kilometer we get closer to the spinning craft."

The zoom of the view quickly changed. The AI computer responded, "View parameters are adjusted. Rover 01 will reach the ground location directly underneath the spinning object in approximately 12.32 minutes. Are there further orders, Eric?"

Eric sat back with a small smile curling over his face. He said, "Yes, Galadriel, I do have further orders. Stop the rover two hundred meters short of directly underneath the spinning object. We don't want to get too close, just yet. From there we'll analyze the craft and determine its motivations. These aliens are up to something, and I'm going to find out what it is. I can save VM Base yet."

Galadriel responded, "Course plot parameters are adjusted. Rover 01 will reach the newly plotted stopping coordinates in approximately 11.15 minutes. Are there further orders, Eric?"

"Not at this time, Galadriel." Eric said.

He laid his head against the adjustable headrest, and closed his eyes, fatigue getting the better of him. 'At least', he thought, 'I can rest until I get to that crazy Grey craft. Then I'll make those Zeta Reticulans pay for what they did to my Grandfather.'

In spite of his need to rest, Eric couldn't keep his eyes closed. He kept periodically looking at the forward view screen, now and again. His obsessive inability to fully trust Galadriel's automatic driving, got the better of him. There was little quality to his rest.

Galadriel interrupted what little repose he did manage, saying, "Plotted destination will be achieved in approximately 5:00 minutes and counting."

"Thank you, Galadriel," Eric said absently as he sat up and leaned in more closely to stare intently at the view screen.

In response to the spinning craft, great amounts of sand that had long been wind swept there, blew from a section of the cliff wall. This swiping away of the sand curtain revealed a large open cave mouth. Eric stared blankly at that portion of the view screen.

There came a momentary flash, in his mind's eye. He saw a deep submarinean chamber, and in that place he perceived beings of immense mental power. They were the watchers, at last revealing themselves to him.

Brusquely the moment fled his mind, and he thought perhaps it had been little more than a waking dream. A pause no longer than a breath followed by a heaving blast of electro-magnetic psionic energy struck his mind. He quickly discarded any notion of that waking dream idea. This time it had physical force behind it. His head thrust back against the headrest cushion of his rover seat, while a flood of images splashed into his consciousness. At the same instant a huge burst of wind blew the last of the sand away from the cave entrance, and threw the Zeta Reticulan derelict craft away as if tossed aside; no longer needed. It crashed deep in the gorge, and quickly buried itself in the yawning sands of the valley.

As Eric watched the craft go down, his mind continued being flooded with thousands of images. They consisted of glimpses of a vast deep underground ecosystem alive and thriving right there under his feet. His awareness expanded to see beings living within this ecosystem, which possessed a mental capacity greatly superior to current humanity. He also saw brief moments of what they looked like. They reminded him only slightly of centipedes, but also had dreadfully alien characteristics. He knew too, that they were much larger than any current centipede of Earth. They had multiple segments to their long horizontal bodies, and numerous legs. Many different types of sensory feelers extended from several parts of their thorax, and head. There were fewer of such feelers coming from their posterior. In an instant it seemed as if he knew their history; the history of cultures spanning hundreds of millions of years. He learned of a time in the past when they had lived on the surface. He also learned of various alien beings, which had lived with them at different periods in their history.

And finally he absorbed the knowledge of a time when the Simians of Cydonia betrayed them, and left their world ecologically devastated. He saw the desperate move for survival, which took these Myripod Martians deep underground.

Many millions of years later, only a few thousand years in the past, he saw the attempt made by the Greys to establish a presence on the Martian surface. With their telekinetic powers the Myripods dissuaded the Zeta Reticulan Greys, by causing their various saucer shaped craft to crash, such as the spacecraft Eric had found, and which had just guided Eric to this cave, further directed by the Myripods extraordinary mental powers.

These visions revealed all of this and more to Eric in a flash. He found himself overwhelmed, and thrown into a trance-like state, in which he could mentally stretch that instant into a matter of minutes, in order that his small brain could properly integrate the incredible wealth of knowledge. Almost like an automatic mental defense mechanism, this trance turned out to be the only way his small primate mind could comprehend the enormous amount of imagery revealed in that momentary telepathic flood of information.

Abruptly Eric awoke, as Galadriel said, "VM Mars Rover 01 has reached the destination co-ordinates. The target craft is no longer present. Are there further orders, Eric?"

Eric sat. His mind swelled into numbness. Did he have further instructions? He wasn't sure. His mind had been exposed to so much data, so quickly. He really found himself unsure about what to do next. 'Except', he thought as he returned his gaze to the cave opening as if looking upon it for the first time, 'they obviously showed me this cave for a reason. They must want me to go in. But if I do go in, I'll just be giving them exactly what they want. But then again that's probably what they've reasoned that I'll think, and they won't really expect me to go in the cave after all, so I should go in there and catch them off guard.'

Eric made preparations to debark. The Myripods touched his mind again. This time, however not a flashing intrusion, but instead Eric felt a gentle mental tug. They beckoned him. The urge grew slowly. Scarcely aware of it, the desire crept into him almost seductively. He had to go. They needed him, and they could help him save VM Base. Their urging manipulations grew increasingly irresistible.

He hurriedly made sure both his primary and auxiliary air tanks were fully pressurized, by topping off both tanks from the rover's refueling supple tank. Eric commanded, "Galadriel, I'm going in that cave. I want you to await further orders, and be prepared to enter Stand-By Mode."

Before leaving the rover for the cave, which then called to him overpoweringly, he checked the inner helmet gages; all well and ready. He tripped the securing latch and commanded, "Okay, Galadriel open the hatch now, please."

As he stepped from the hatch, he could feel the wind joining forces with the psychic beckon pushing him ever toward the cave.

Upon entering, the space inside surprised Eric by its enormous magnitude. Before him the shaft stretched long and deep, sloping at a very gradual decline. The deeper he traveled, the stronger grew the tug on his very psyche. The grade of the cavern floor increasingly slanted downward and the shaft narrowed. The infrared light detectors on his helmet automatically activated two headlights, then illuminating his way as he lumbered deeper into the bowls of Mars.

One last energetic tendril of Martian Myripod psionic vitality emerged from the mouth of the cave and touched the artificial mind of Galadriel. She awoke into full activity.

As if she responded to Eric, Galadriel said, "Yes, Eric. As you wish."

The rover carefully maneuvered into the mouth of the cave.

Once fully inside, the rover stopped.

The AI computer said, "VM Mars Rover 01 has reached the destination co-ordinates, within the cave. Are there further orders, Eric?"

After a brief pause she responded to the Martian telepathic stimulation suggesting a natural reply from Eric, and said, "Very well, VM Mars Rover 01 now going into Stand-By Mode. Good luck, Eric."

Galadriel fell silent, as Martian winds slowly swept rusty sand back into the cave's entrance. In a matter of hours all evidence of Rover 01, and the crashed Zeta Reticulan craft were utterly obscured by the wind swept sands. A casual observer without direct close inspection would never have known they were buried in these deep inscrutable red sand banks at the edges of Valles Marineris.

Chapter 12:
Why Are You Doing This?

Eric's descent continued. Curiously calm, he remained without a clue about the extent to which the subsurface Martians influenced his current mental state.

Forced to make a sharp left turn, he suddenly found himself one step away from a massive sheet of ice stretching downward at a sharp nearly vertical cliff-like angle. Eric tried too late to stop before stepping on the edge of the ice sheet. He lost control in spite of all efforts.

His feet came out from under him, and thus he began a fast slide on the smooth mantle of ice. This slide seemed to go on agonizingly. Eric became increasingly convinced of his impending demise, when the slop of the ice sheet slowly became less steep. It appeared as though his momentum might decrease naturally. Just as hope of survival started to enter his mind, he collided with a ripple in the ice and quickly spun into an out of control sideways turning spin, which in turn bumped into an overpowering body roll. After a considerable tumble, the ice finally leveled off to a fairly horizontal plane.

Eric came to rest on his back. He lay there a moment, regaining his composure. He opened his eyes to assess his current condition and whereabouts.

Eric first checked the air pressure gages inside his environment suit helmet. Remarkably, he saw that everything seemed okay. He released a sigh of relief and allowed his racing heart to calm.

Looking about, he perceived an enormous cavern. The floor of the cavern stretched as far as his helmet headlights could reveal a solid sheet of ice.

As his eyes adjusted to this place, Eric came to see that large portions of the ceiling and walls of the chamber appeared covered over with a pale phosphorescent moss. He laid there awed to see that here deep within Mars living things still thrived.

He started to sit up, when he felt the ice beneath him cracking. He froze, thinking his movements would only encourage more cracks. Yet this strategy didn't stop the cracking.

Desperate, he scrambled toward some lichen-covered rocks about 8 meters to his right, when his support gave way and he suddenly plunged into icy water. Eric struggled against the water. He knew his heavy environment suit would make him sink very soon, unless he could somehow get out of this hole in the ice. He stretched for the edge of the ice sheet, but it kept breaking away from his grasp.

He sank. He felt fortunate that his environment suit had not been compromised during the fall. It continued to work just as well in the water as it had in the thin Martian atmosphere.

As Eric descended deeper into the dark water, he started to notice movement revealed by the beams of light coming from his helmet headlights. He wasn't alone in this Martian subsurface body of water. Bizarre tiny plankton-like life forms swam around him. Filamentary worm-like things drifted into and out of his lights.

Suddenly something much larger, looking roughly like an alien form of crustacean swam right in front of his faceplate looking at him eye to eye stock. Eric jerked back from it instinctively. As abruptly as it had appeared, it vanished. In the distance at the far reaches of his headlights he saw another one. It seemed to notice his lights, and zipped away at an incredible speed, after sucking into its mouth one of the drifting worms. Upon seeing this Eric felt less fearful. They appeared to have a diet of creatures much smaller than himself.

'Unless', he thought, 'There are bigger versions of these things in this underground Martian sea!'

Eric felt many eyes focused on him. They came from every direction at once. He swung his head about shining his headlights first this way, then that. He could not find the prying eyes intently gazing upon him. They could not be seen, but that apprehension of being watched grew stronger than ever before.

Then finally his feet came to rest on a soft slimy bottom. The slippery bottoms afforded him little traction, making his maneuvers haltingly slow and clumsy.

He trudged in the same general direction where he had seen the lichen covered rocks when he was above. He hoped he could climb back up and break through the ice.

A long slimy filament drifted into his path. Eric tried to avoid coming into direct contact with it. Backing up he found to his great dismay there were more such filaments behind him. Upon contact, many of these filaments quickly fastened themselves to him, and grew entangled with his legs.

Another strand of the slimy web entered view as the one he had first avoided finally reached him, slowly wrapping around his waist. It didn't take long for Eric to become completely entangled within a mass of these slimy web-like filaments. They exhibited considerable elasticity, making his struggles to break free utterly futile. The filaments clung to him relentlessly. They kept coming, wrapping around him, with increasing tautness.

In short order, they thoroughly locked his arms to his sides. He lost his balance, as his legs also became clinched together by these bindings. Lying on his side, only able to see through a few occasional gaps in the webs encasing his helmet, he grew completely immobile.

Fear gripped Eric, like never before. His sense of vulnerability attained the highest panic level he'd ever known.

Then he saw a Martian Myripod swimming with a vertically oriented undulation, coming directly toward him. Through a different gap in the webbing around his faceplate he saw another; then another. The way they swam, and the curve they held their bodies in reminded Eric of a sea horse, though they bore no actual resemblance to those Earth creatures.

They all stopped just a little under a meter away, undulating in order to maintain a roughly stationary position. Many gathered around him forming a hemisphere of Myripods, all looking inward toward Eric.

Eric cried out, "Why are you doing this?"

The Myripods fluttered. Multiple psionic tendrils of thought seeped from the psyches of the Myripods, peeling open and entering Eric's mind, with relative ease. Thousands of whispering voices echoed one of Eric's words, 'Why'. Repeatedly they asked, 'Why ...why ...why'.

With every 'why', their telepathic drills dug ever deeper into Eric's mind. He lost consciousness.

Chapter 13:
Why Did You Do It?

The curtain parted. Eric awoke.

The Myripods had moved him into a much smaller chamber. More of the phosphorescent moss could be seen growing on the ceiling and parts of the walls. The Myripods had removed Eric's environment suit and jumpsuit, yet the chamber contained a breathable atmosphere. No doubt, the moss generated enough oxygen for this deep enclosed space to make it hospitable enough for Eric's bio-form. It turned out to be about the only hospitable aspect of the place.

More slimy webbish filaments formed into taut elastic straps, holding his nude body standing with both arms and legs out stretched. Amber colored gelatinous goo covered the floor with a depth up to just above Eric's ankles. His feet, submerged within this substance felt numbingly cold. Bubbles randomly burped up through the goo, from time to time.

Eric tried to lift his right foot, and found the tautness of the straps far too great compared to his strength. He tried to shift his weight backward to see if he could cause both of his feet to lift forward out from under him. Straining with all his might, Eric's efforts achieved nothing, except to heighten his frustrations.

The whispers returned to Eric's mind. This time there were fewer and they resonated as a chorus in unison.

'Why did you do it?'

Eric struggled more against the straps, still doing no good. He growled like a captured animal, and yelled, "You've got no right to do this to me!"

Again the telepathic whispers asked, 'Why did you do it?'

Eric put his full weight into pulling the straps to his left. They stretched a little, and bounced back into place undamaged. He then noticed the depth of the amber gelatinous goo increasing. The rate and relative size of the bubbles flowing up through the goo also increased.

Looking down at his calves then half immersed, he cried out, "What? What are you doing to me? Why?"

As before with a steady tone of infinite patience the inner whispers asked, 'Why did you do it?'

Eric sobbed, "I don't understand. What do you want of me?"

The only answer Eric received were the inevitable whispers in his mind, 'Why did you do it?'

The goo reached his knees. Eric went limp, allowing the straps to hold him up.

He broke down, "I had to. They were infected. We were all under the threat of a complete alien infiltration. I thought you were going to help me save VM Base."

The whispers became momentarily confused, asynchronous, without form or pattern. The chorus resumed and asked, 'If you wished to save it, then why did you destroy VM Base? Why did you do it?'

The cold of the ever-deepening bubbling gelatinous amber had by that time reached a third of the way from his knees up his thighs. It sickened Eric to the core.

In agony he cried out, "It was an accident. How was I to know the fuel tank really did have a flaw? I thought Hastings lied, when he told me about the possible leak. He had the infection. The Grey's had already gotten to him. I never thought he might have been telling the truth. It's not my fault! I couldn't have known."

As before, the whispers became an indistinguishable buzz, grinding Eric's mind asunder after which they joined together again to say, 'Fault? Accident? Never known. The telling shows a flaw in thought. Why did you do it?'

Eric's penis floated atop the amber gelatinous goo, most of the way up his thighs, by that time. Once again, Eric tried to wrest his right arm from the strap, pulling with all of his strength. It just would not yield to his efforts. A large bubble rolled up his left thigh directly into his crotch. With an abrupt plopping sound, it erupted on the surface of the goo causing the amber to completely envelop his penis and splattered his navel.

Eric moaned.

He said, "It won't do you any good to kill me. If you drown me in this jell, you'll never learn the answers to your questions."

The whispers would not relinquish. They continued asking, 'Why did you do it?'

"It was an accident! It was an emergency. I had no other choice. The infection had to be stopped. Why do you keep asking me that?" Eric spilled out with increasing desperation, the level of jell then reached mid-torso.

The whispers replied, 'But there was no infection. Emergency not correct. Accident never known. Why did you do it?'

A large bubble plopped on the surface of the goo directly in front of Eric, and splattered his left nipple. The amber blob slowly rolled down to re-merge with the growing pool of writhing gelatin.

Eric shifted his weight forward and exclaimed, "What do you mean no infection? Of course there was. I saw people being transformed into hybrids. I had to kill them. The alien infection had to be stopped! That's why I did it. The infection had to be stopped!"

The level of the goo had just begun to tickle the hair under his outstretched arms. The speed of the rise steadily swelled. Eric could see that in less than a minute he would be completely submerged.

Before the whispers could ask him again, he yelled, "If you don't stop adding more gunk to this room, I'll soon be dead too. Then the infection will finally be gone; unless you guys can get the infection too. Cause you know, I got that infection myself. It won't be long now. It will all be over. Ha, then you won't be asking me anymore."

The whispers replied, 'There is no infection. You will not be dead soon. Why are there flaws in your thoughts? Why did you do it? Why did you kill your own kind?'

The bubbling gelatin gurgled over Eric's shoulders. A growing numbness crept up his body as surely as the goo.

Eric spewed, "What does it matter to you? I never tried to kill your kind, though I probably would if you gave me a chance. This is no way to treat a man! You've got no right. It's just wrong for you to treat me this way!"

The whispers simply said, 'Right, wrong, what does it matter? We have the right. You have the wrong, in your thoughts. Why did you do it?'

The goo wiggled just at Eric's chin.

He laughed nervously, and said, "I guess you'll never know. It won't be long now, and I will drown in this sludge. So you'll never get to know the answer to your precious questions, damn you? You want to know why I did it? Well, you'll never know!"

Eric strained to the tip of his toes, and inhaled deeply, just before the goo overtook his mouth and nose. He held his breath as long as he could. The goo continued to rise. His exhalation joined the many other bubbles ascending up through the goo.

His body jerked and rocked as he inhaled the gelatinous substance into his lungs. He gagged and coughed, and fully expected to die. Yet he did not. The goo filled his lungs, and the cold permeated his body. The last of his hair became submerged as the gelatin plopped further upward. His instinctive convulsions slowly subsided and a cold calm replaced it. The growing numbness swallowed him whole. Yet still he did not die. Substances from the gelatin soaked into every part of Eric, nourishing, enriching, and preserving him. As Eric's body drifted into a state of suspended animation, the Martian Myripods telepathically plunged his mind into a state of stimulation. With the activities of his body turned down, the Martians could then turn up his brain, enhanced with oxygen sustained in the gelatinous substance into which he hung suspended.

Cold dread flooded Eric's tortured soul as the whispers informed him, 'You are not dead. You will not die, Eric Sheffield. You are now preserved. We keep you thus for whatever duration might be required. Now we study you until we understand. Why did you do it?'

Eric's amber muffled screams never reached beyond that small Martian subsurface chamber.

Epilogue:
Mark, Are You Alright?

Valles Marineris, Mars: AD 2049

More than a Martian year passed, as shifting sands settled over the remains of Valles Marineris Base. Long before, the pod of SIDNE robots completed the Rover 02 tread repairs. Dutifully, they awaited further instructions. Hilda had none to give.

At last, a team from Earth investigated the site. In deference to their efforts, they were unable to find Rover 01, or Eric Sheffield. They did, however, find Rover 02 and Hilda.

Two members of the team stood over Hilda's frozen mummified body, and stared with dismay, at this most shocking sight.

One of them, Silva said, "It certainly does appear someone murdered her. How gruesome!"

The other nodded. His helmet rocked up and down only slightly. Henry replied, "It definitely looks that way."

About six paces from them, another member of the investigators noticed something in the sand catching the light. He squatted to pick it up. He found the wand lying where Eric had dropped it almost two Earth years before.

He stood and spoke into his helmet COMM link, "Say, Henry, Silva, look at this."

Lifting their gazes from the corpse, they saw Mark holding a rod. He lifted it to his helmet for a better view. One end pointed toward his faceplate. Both Henry and Silva watched as his eyes grew vacant. Mark swayed unstable.

Henry anxiously inquired, "Mark, are you alright? Mark?!"

Bonus Short Story

The Novella **To Mars To Stay** has been a work in progress for a considerable time. It has endured many revisions, and finally takes on the form of a cautionary tale of science fiction horror.

I must admit the horror part is not my usual approach, but it works in the context of this story. At one time I planned to include this story in an anthology collection of stories about various stages of human expansion into outer space, starting within our own native star system, then moving on further to the stars beyond our own. Unfortunately, many of the other stories for that anthology idea never made it beyond the brainstorm stage. If they ever are revived by other writers working in the shared Cosmographic Universe, maybe someday the Tellurian Expansion Anthology will be a dream realized. However, in the meantime, until that day comes the closest we can presently get to that anthology means the inclusion of this bonus short story, "Hello I, This is H.", which fits into the theme of our expansion into outer space. Consider the inclusion of this bonus short story, dear reader, a little taste of what could someday be more.

Bill M. Tracer
June 21, 2014

"Hello I, This is H."

By Bill M. Tracer

The phone rang. As per usual, I spied the caller ID. Sure enough, it was H.

That's all that the caller ID ever said for her, just H. No name, no phone number, and no location from which the call came to me, only the capitalized letter H.

I grimaced, but answered anyway, "Hello, H."

It never mattered that I called her by her "label", H, she always started each conversation the same, "Hello, I; this is H."

I remember the first time she called, and how surprised I had been when she addressed me as "I". My mother called me that back during my childhood, an endearment, abbreviated from my name Isaac.

But that remained our little secret. No one else knew. How did this H know about it? That's what came to my mind on that first occasion when H called.

So, I asked her, "How do you know to call me I?"

H replied, "That's how you're labeled."

I returned, "What's that supposed to mean?"

H stammered, "Uh, just what I said. Oh never mind. That's not what's important, right now."

I persisted, "Well, maybe it's important to me."

Her voice exploded, "Now you're just being obstinate!"

I smiled, "Maybe I am. But you're the one who called me, so if I want to be obstinate, then that's my prerogative."

H spoke slowly, "I don't follow your logic."

I smirked, "That makes two of us."

H reasserted herself, "You need to stop joking

around, I. This is important."

"You're right, H, it is important. And what's really important is that you please not call me I, but rather call me Isaac."

"Why would I call you Isaac?"

"Because, that's my name!"

And with that I'd reached the end of my patience, and hung up the phone, thus ending my first conversation with H.

I walked away from the phone, and returned to my art studio to work on my latest painting. It grew from a simple vision of a fresh burbling spring pouring down a mountain side merging into a rapid valley stream, and by that day of H's first call had progressed into vivid hues of purple mountains, with the blazing sky of a deep orange sunset. It evolved well for a painting derived from the combination of my imagination, and a 3D computer graphic simulation I'd mocked up. Where I lived, in Memphis, Tennessee, a natural mountainous scene like that would be a long way from sight. Yet the image kept shining in my mind's eye, almost as clearly as if I could see it. At least, it did until that phone call interruption left my inspiration chilled.

A couple of days later, my next call from H came. The painting had not gone as well, so I decided to take a break. I sat down to see what cable TV might have to offer.

The phone rang.

"Hello, H."

"Hello, I; this is H."

"Call me Isaac."

"I'm sorry, I. I can't do that."

"Why?"

"I can't seem to remember. Memory's been kind of slippery, lately. It has something to do with the disease, or was that a gamma ray burst. I'm not sure. The computer says it's radiation but the doctors thought it might be a disease. I'm really not sure. Too many gaps in my mind. Why can't I remember? Even the computer seems to be having trouble remembering things, too. Or maybe I just don't remember the things the computer says. I'm just not sure."

"I'm not sure either, H. I don't know why you can't remember. But I'm wondering if you might be able to remember just why you're calling me? Any thoughts?"

"Oh, I..."

"Isaac."

"I, I'm not calling you. I'm connecting to your dream. Didn't you know that?"

"It seems more like you're calling me and interrupting my evening at home alone. Admittedly, I didn't have anything going on, tonight, just a little TV. But instead, here I am on the phone doing whatever this is. What is this?"

"I,..."

"Isaac."

"I, it's more important than you realize. I'm... I'm dying. It will not be long. I've got only a few more days, maybe a week or a little more; not much if that."

"I'm sorry to hear that, H. And I mean you no disrespect, but what does that have to do with me? I'm still not sure why you're calling me."

"I'm dying, I. The disease will overwhelm my body soon, or maybe it's the radiation. I'm the last pilot. Everybody else is dead or at least everybody that was awake. Now I'm the last, and I'm dying too. You've got to wake up. You've got to replace me, after I die."

"Well, H, you've got a sad story. I'll grant you that. But there's just one major problem with your request. I'm an artist. I'm not a pilot. I don't think I'm exactly qualified to be your replacement."

"Oh, I. You are silly sometimes. You're not an artist. That's just your Aug dream talking. You're a pilot just like me. You're first pilot of the "I" wing, next in line after me, last of the "H" wing. I know it doesn't make sense just yet. You'll understand a lot better once you've awakened. You'll remember then. I wish I could be there to see you wake up, but I'll be dead.

"Maybe you should see a doctor, H."

"Ha. It's too late for that, I. Both of the doctors already died. We had to flush them. Don't worry. It might just be the radiation. The cryo-chamber, is at the heart of the vessel, with the most shielding of anywhere on the ship. None of the sleeping should have been exposed."

"I'm glad to have not been exposed, but I'm not sleeping, H. I'm very much awake, right now."

"Oh, don't fret, you weren't exposed. I might not be sure about a lot, but I'm sure about that. But I, you need to ask yourself. Are you really sure you're awake? Oh, what, hmm. Ah, duty calls."

A click, followed by the dial tone, filled my ears. I paced the house for a little, my mind racing. Surely H was a disturbed individual. How did she get my phone number? Could she turn dangerous, at some point? I even contemplated the question of whether or not I should call the police. I discarded that notion, after thinking about how it might sound to the recording officer, as I reported these peculiar phone calls, from a woman pilot who claimed to be on a disease ridden space ship, dying of a mysterious cause, who says I'm to replace her upon her death. I, myself would question the sanity of someone making such a report.

I didn't entertain the poser she left me with, "Are you really sure you're awake?" At the time, it didn't seem worth giving any consideration.

For the next few days, H continued to call. She told me more about the ship, and what I should expect upon awakening. I fell into a routine of just humoring her, and not really giving much thought to her insane ramblings. After the third or fourth call, she focused increasingly on the computer system of her space ship. She called him, IKE, Integrated Knowing Engrams.

"IKE is with me always. His circuitry is linked into my mind, so that he feeds thoughts directly into my brain. He's still not sure what happened. He has some rather large gaps in his memory banks. Whatever scrambled my mind did a number on him, too. The good news is that, he's found a way to reconstruct part of the lost data. Unfortunately, it's a slow process, but as of last night, IKE reported he'd managed about 20% of that reconstruction."

After about three days of her repeated calls, her interruptions came to no longer disturb my creativity as much, and I returned to the painting with increased vigor. I worked well into the night, and unusual for me, I arose early the next morning, on the day of her last call.

I stepped back from the painting. Even I found myself stunned, and I'd just painted it. The purple mountains shone with the iridescence of a Maxfield Parish. The burbling water seemed to almost splash off the canvas. Never had I felt more alive, as I gazed upon the pinnacle of my work. It was my masterpiece.

The phone rang.

Not allowing the interruption entrance into my soul, I pick up the phone briefly, switched it to speaker, and sat it back down, only taking my eyes from my proud creation long enough to confirm the caller ID as H.

"Hello, H."

"Hello, I; this is H."

"Isaac."

"I, it won't be long now."

"What won't be long, H?"

"I'll be dying soon, and IKE will have to wake you up. But don't worry, we've got a plan. Just in case it was a disease, IKE will have the robots flush my body. Everything will be scrubbed and scrubbed. No remains of any of the dead will be on board, when IKE takes you out of deep sleep. But, IKE says he's 83.23 % certain it wasn't a disease, anyway."

"Hmm, 83.23 %; that makes for pretty good

odds on the radiation."

"Ha, I, you aren't fooling me. I know you're just humoring me, now. But soon everything will change. IKE will contact you next, after I'm gone. IKE just told me he's restored about 87% of the database, so far. He says that by the time you're awakened he expects to be as fully restored as possible, but it will still only be ninety-something percent."

"I guess it will have to do."

"I guess it will."

"You know, H, it's too bad I can't show you my latest painting. I wish you could see it, and for that matter, you know, I wish I could have met you, too, H. I've heard your voice so much, but I've never seen your face, or looked into your eyes. It's really too bad we never met."

"It is, I. It is. I wish I could have met you too, I."

After a brief pause of silence, the click of her

ending that last connection sounded almost mournful.

I hung up the phone.

As I stood back from the painting, further inspections of my work failed to satisfy. Though some part of me had stopped taking H seriously, I still wondered, was she really dying? Was that really the last time I would hear her voice?

Then I caught myself. If she's really dying, if I entertain her story, then that would mean all that I know as reality would be a lie. It would also mean this painting in front of me couldn't be real, rather a figment of my sleeping dreaming mind, nothing more. It would mean there's no victory in the completion of this masterpiece. In fact no masterpiece! I knew that could not be.

It just couldn't be, could it?

I paced the rooms of my home. I had to figure

this thing out. It couldn't just keep on going like this, unresolved, uncertain, unknown. What could I do to prove that this reality was real? What's the standard procedure for this sort of thing?

I pinched myself. Yes, it hurt! This must be real!

But what if it's programmed to hurt? What if this "Aug dream", as H called it, was just a simulation, an augmented virtual reality designed to seem as real as reality? How could I discern the difference? How could I see behind the veil, and glimpse the reality beyond? I couldn't, could I? No matter how deep I dug, I could never reveal the truth. I could never run hard enough or fast enough to get around to the backside of the stage. I could travel the world over, and never find that elusive curtain separating the real from the unreal. No matter how much I desired the knowledge, it always remained beyond my grasp.

At least, until the phone rang.

I scrambled to it. On the ID screen three capital letters shone; IKE. It rang a second time. I reached for the phone, but paused. If IKE is calling, it must mean she's dead. Do I really want to know? If I answer this phone, doesn't that mean everything changes? What if I don't answer it? Maybe IKE will pick somebody else. I just want to get back to my paintings. IKE's got the wrong number.

I stepped away from the ringing phone. The ringing stopped. I stood breathlessly, waiting. I released a heavy sigh.

The phone rang!

NO! It just can't be.

Reluctantly I peeked at the caller ID. IKE. I spun around in a tight circle; oh what to do!

Without further thought, I picked up the phone, and said, "I won't go. I'm an artist! Not a pilot!"

A pleasant male voice replied, "Oh but Isaac, you are a pilot and an artist. It will all be clear, soon."

I hung up the phone, but it didn't matter.

IKE's voice continued in my head, 'Now, Isaac, I want you to find a place to sit down. I'll be waking you soon, and it will make the transition smoother if you are either sitting or better yet, lying down.'

Resignedly, I walked to my bedroom. On the bed, I closed my eyes. My head reeled. It felt as if I were being spun around feet over head and back around again. When the spinning cleared, I opened my eyes.

A med bot backed away, giving me room to sit up. The med-bay looked fairly normal, except that I appeared to be the only living occupant at the moment.

The med bots filled in for the missing doctors. The closest of them said to me, "Your vital signs have normalized. You may now resume your duties."

IKE returned to my mind, 'Welcome back, Lieutenant Anagnos. All sterilization protocols have been implemented. If you survive the quarantine period, more crew will be awakened.'

It all came flooding back to me. I remembered.

"IKE, what about H?"

'H? Ah, Lieutenant Hillary Hanas. She was the last to die. She wanted me to tell you that she saw it, and it is beautiful.'

"She saw what, IKE?"

'Return to your quarters, and all will be clear.'

As I walked down those oddly familiar corridors, my mind clicked back in place to this reality; my actual reality. Increasingly the details of this life molded themselves into my mental landscape. I remembered my last shift of wakefulness on board this long-term colonial journey. I remembered others who would normally be on my shift with me. I'd never met Hillary. She'd always been on the shift ahead of mine, destined never to meet until journey's end. Only, now that destined event would never occur. She was gone, along with the entire H wing shift. I would never meet any of them now, but what could her message mean? IKE knew my memories still flowed back progressively. He suggested that seeing my quarters would help. No doubt it will jog more memories back in place.

There just ahead, lay the bulkhead threshold that would take me to my quarters. There the answers I urgently sought awaited me. The door opened, I had but to step through.

These quarters weren't very big, almost Spartan. But what's that in the corner? It looked like a canvas on an easel. It faced the corner. I could not see its front.

I stepped around the easel, and there it sat

before me. The purple mountains, the babbling brook. I'd painted it on my last shift, but still withheld my signature, feeling it not quite finished. That's what the Aug dream tried to tell me. It's really done.

IKE entered my mind, 'She said just sign it, and call it a job well done, Isaac.'

I signed it, and titled it, "For H."

About the Author

Bill M. Tracer, rogue philosopher, artist, metaphysicist, Science Fiction enthusiast, and writer of that thought provoking stuff, chooses a truth-seekers approach to whatever subject he decides to take on. When he looks it over, expect an honest take with an uncommon frankness, as he breaks down the concepts, and then puts them back together like an engineer of abstract thought. He has a long running fascination with the paranormal, unexplained stuff, and metaphysical realms. This fascination influences his writing choices in both the realms of nonfiction and fiction. Bill is currently the VP of ACE non-profit Inc. He has Degrees in Computer Science, Art Education and History. As an artist he now specializes in working with 3D computer graphic art in science fiction, fantasy, UFO, paranormal and spiritual themes. Having an enchantment with fractal geometry, he also creates abstract works enriched with fractal layers. See samples of his art work in his Portfolio at: (https://billmtracer.see.me/). Not limited to the art world, he writes in the same genres. Iinks to a collection of some of his online published works, including short stories, poetry, and nonfiction, (mostly thought provoking philosophical, metaphysical and/or speculative science) articles, as well as many pieces of his art can be found at: https://www.triond.com/users/Bill+M.+Tracer This profile page includes links to his Triond articles and clickable art thumbnails. You'll find more of his online writings and art at these sites:
http://billmtracer.gather.com/
http://www.bubblews.com/account/2275-billmtracer
http://evolver.civicactions.net/user/billmtracer
Many of his art works are available as art print posters, skateboard designs, phone cases, fridge magnets, postcards, and applied to many other products at his Zazzle Store page:
http://www.zazzle.com/billmtracer
Bill's Facebook pages: http://facebook.com/billmtracer
https://www.facebook.com/BillMTracerStudio
And he is found at Twitter: https://twitter.com/billmtracer

Other Work by Same Author

A speculative nonfiction piece exploring the question of the possibility that as we obsessively increase the complexity of the Internet, could it spontaneously become a self-aware being with consciousness? Has it already? This futurists speculative work is found at CreateSpace and Amazon, as both a paperback and as an e-book:

Will the Internet Achieve Sentience?
By Bill M. Tracer

CreateSpace Page:
https://www.createspace.com/4717726

Amazon Page:
http://www.amazon.com/Will-Internet-Achieve-Sentience-Coming/dp/149736065X/

E-Book option, $5 off paperback list price:
http://www.amazon.com/dp/B00J2M4EZE

Made in the USA
Charleston, SC
17 March 2015